The Drift That Follows Will Be Gradual

A Novel

Alan Rifkin

OPEN
BOOKS

Published by Open Books

Copyright © 2024 by Alan Rifkin

Interior Design by Siva Ram Maganti

Cover image © by Pics Garden shutterstock.com/g/msr+meloool

Advance Praise for
The Drift That Follows Will Be Gradual

"A delectable tour de force through our fractured culture from the 1980s through the 2010s—it is witty, wise, memorable, touching, by turns drop dead funny and piercingly moving. You won't soon forget Richard Leviton, his troubled son Philip, or Bailey Kavanagh, Leviton's nurturer and conscience in her way, a wonderfully realized woman whose best trait is her capacity for love. This is a wonderful book. Delicious all the way through."

—Richard Bausch

"I was seduced by the heartbreaking, soul-warming chapters in *The Drift That Follows Will Be Gradual*. The fine balance of tenderness and toughness in Rifkin's voice began to feel like part of my own. Every bit of this book feels like a new best friend."

—Meg Pokrass, author of
The First Law of Holes: New and Selected Stories

"Rifkin's crisp dialog and masterful scene setting eased me instantly into 'the most fascinating city in the world' and the souls of his young and then not-so-young characters as they quest and fumble their way through artist, musician and mainly writer lives in late 20th and early 21st Century Los Angeles. The often aphoristic clarity of his observations stirs awe. His narrator hints at why that is: 'Sometimes I think that all along, when I was clinging with such weird, vicarious self regard to what felt special about coming alive in the 1980s, I was trying to pilfer a taste of it for this future son.' This son develops mental illness. As it intensifies, I felt increasingly grateful that the novel allowed me, too, to follow the protagonist's struggle to decipher Los

Angeles while decoding the alternate but probably no more weird reality in his beloved child's mind."

—Bob Sipchen, Pulitzer Prize-winning
journalist and author of *Baby Insane and the Buddha*

Contents

2015

Is a delusion like one of those extra rooms you discover in a dream? Once you've seen the room, then all the floorplans that hide it are conspiracies. The fact the room can't be proved is the proof of the room. Over time, Philip has grown tired of having to explain this to me, humbled by the genius of his enemies.

Paper Moon: 1985

———◆———

IT WAS EXACTLY THE right hour to pass groups of twenty-somethings leaving the bars, which was one of the comforts of 1985 in Los Angeles. The women dressed so much smarter than the men it made them look lonely, like girls too tall in sixth grade. Bailey was past thirty but wore an army jacket with a white work shirt untucked like a boy's and cigarette jeans she was too wide for, half youth cadet, half spinster, and I said I'd drive her home from Ports because she was the city's "designated non-driver," one of my better tries at being witty back then, but it never stuck. When she first arrived from DC she actually bought a car, but she resold it to the dealer the next week, and despite the impossibility of getting around LA except by cab, she never wavered.

We were in the dirt lot air outside the Pan Pacific Theatre's ruins looking for wherever my car had been last, leaving the ghostly senora who owned Ports framed in the doorway of the bar.

Bailey's voice kept shivering though it wasn't cold out. "*Ohh, is that what sagebrush smells like?*"

I grunted—to show that names of plants were charmingly out of my male reach, always wishing I could be a lug instead of a writer. And when I didn't say more, she tried to take responsibility for missing my meaning, with a slow, catching-on laugh. I always had the benefit of the doubt with Bailey.

A legend about Bailey Kavanagh was that at age six, on a swing set in South Carolina, she promised never to get married or have kids, chanting NO KIDS every time the chain lurched skyward. But she could not recall a triggering event. It didn't help to ask, because what Bailey didn't know about herself, she didn't know. And despite how unimportant she considered herself to be, she could shut down a topic with as little apology as a White House spokeswoman.

At the magazine where Bailey championed other people's creativity all day, the first story I wrote was about growing up so sheltered in the San Fernando Valley that I asked for a Buick Riviera from a Christmas charity. The piece, in 1983, went through a lot of less honest drafts before the mortifying truth finally pierced her. That plus a poor-fitting pair of slacks I'd bought on Hollywood Boulevard the same day, from a touristy clothier who had shoe-polish ads in the window. I strode into his store against every pulsing neon omen, determined to believe he could make me look more substantial than LA. Bailey asked if I wore the slacks to make girls swoon—like that, we were on my turf.

And when I realized she might have a crush, not just on my writing, my wires were as disconnected as hers. She was material for what I drank to as the legend of my twenties, about being a young bylined writer—my name is Richard Leviton—in what people would someday agree was the most fascinating city in the world.

My father's generation had adulthood forced upon them, the Great Depression, a world war, then hedonism, and there was something hermetic about his car and the songbook of his life, in his generation's outstanding talent for driving more slowly than all the other lanes—I used to see all of Ronald Reagan's deinstitutionalized phantoms stirring in their blankets when my dad drove us past them, their eyes looking for mine, but I wanted only to be glib in 1985.

Inside her upper duplex, Bailey switched on a light and opened all the windows and slid into a reclining chair that was bean-bag low, making her look like the drunk one of us, and started right in channeling questions from the ceiling. "How do writers do it?" she

3

marveled at one point. "Do they all go crazy about breaking paragraphs in the perfect spot?"

At work, she'd sometimes hear Stephen Bates pounding on the walls of a typing room to get out a story—which I said made perfect sense: Didn't he throw a party at his girlfriend's house in the hills every time he finished anything? I'd been invited to one, filled with smart, sexy Stephen-groupies—magazine writers had swag in 1985—and his quotable aside that night was, "You know how many wrong directions a first sentence can go? Infinity—I counted."

"*Wait*," Bailey pouted, stuck one beat behind. "How does someone get to be a 'smart, sexy' woman?"

I volunteered Katherine Hepburn's advice: Use good posture and think dirty thoughts. But that only made Bailey sadder—it would never be her style.

She kept playing this tragic game of footsie. Why did her best friend take a stranger into the bathroom stall to fuck? Why did Bailey's first boyfriend laugh with her about all the guys from the art department drawn to the troubled, sexpot intern, only to fall in bed with her himself?

The lure of the wrong! in other words. And the cruelty of nature. *Was everyone like that?* She was asking this in a writerly, student-of-life way—not that it ruled out feeling wounded when that boyfriend betrayed her. And enough men whom she liked had left parties with Bailey's sister's number that Bailey essentially stopped talking to men at parties.

It was late enough or I was drunk enough to marvel at things without talking, just to slump into Bailey's no-fault world, when she said, "Have you ever made love to a fat girl?"

So we did. To say I was honoring the sacredness of the proposition would be giving me too much credit. In my twenties, I didn't know men could say no. She leaned over me and we kissed, and the hardness of her kiss felt fresh, like it might hurt in a good way later. Almost immediately we were in the hallway, shuffling sidewise between towers of books, until she was turning on a bright papier-mâché lantern that was her night lamp. "Yes?" she asked. "We really are?"

4

It felt less presumptuous to unbutton her shirt than my own, I don't know why. She was thick and round, which I already knew, but firmer than I was worried she'd be. Velvety, figureless. When I got to my undershirt, she admired each phase. "You're so long!"

That got me going, well enough for her to climb on top with me inside her. But then the novelty cruelly faded. With each jolt, a ghost of faith was shaken loose, and we were both bouncing, half passed out, with me silently praying to start over. There are no atheists in a bedroom that has lost the orchestra.

"I shouldn't have forced things," she said. "You were being kind."

"No," I said. Which was true: The only ego I'd been concerned about was mine.

But I watched her take hope from the perfectly rational idea that there'd be plenty more chances in bed. "Agh!" she said, and bounced to her feet, wrestling her way into the thin black jeans. "You've at least got to take some of these books off my hands."

Into a canvas bag, she slid all the right things—a couple of advance-reader galleys of novels, a paperback manual on Zen, and a clip of manuscript pages by a hotshot writer named Cody Castille, who she said should meet me (although of course it was the other way around). But when she moved toward some art books, I almost insulted her. "Seriously," I said. "I'm tone-deaf to paintings." Painting was Bailey's hobby. "I mean, some photography speaks to me, the way photos can make all of us look like lost souls. But with paintings?" I went further. "Do men even go to museums by choice? Why go to stare at paintings in a gallery when you can stare as long as you want to in a book?"

"Because they're the right size?"

Her answer came out so free of malice, like a guess, that we both burst out laughing, and that was that. This was how it was with Bailey: You could believe that none of your missteps affected how likable you were. If she was a genius about editing, why not people?

So I drove home with the book bag next to me, thinking how much better it was to have a care package from Bailey than from any of the people who raised me. It was soul food for my newly imagined self. Not that she had any special access to my dreams. For people who'd failed in bed, we weren't that comfortable being friends, either. Though, for that reason alone, our connection felt more important than just a friendship. And, after all, I hadn't technically shut the door on a relationship.

———————

Cody Castille was perfectly named, everyone said, like someone from a tall tale. His jaw was beautiful, his skin golden, and his ears tipped back like a steer's. He even came from New Mexico, but that was all the childhood you'd ever hear from him, even though he talked so constantly the word *garrulous* appeared in every news item that ever mentioned him. If Cody went missing, you'd tell police to look for somebody garrulous.

Only twenty-five, he'd dazzled everyone, New York editors, famous rappers, music journalism prize committees, but he also made it a point to offend them. Riding over to his place, Bailey told me Cody only did what most of his editors fantasized doing—insisting his stories run verbatim or not at all, and being fine if they refused, to the point of laughing through his nose.

We sat on folding chairs at sundown in his small but high-ceilinged living room, waiting for gumbo, me constantly tugging my pant legs to cover my socks, not convinced the dorkiness could make anyone swoon but Bailey. Cody's painter girlfriend, Dehlia, had the whole couch, and she sat tall in the center, a bright package no one had claimed. She had haunted eyes and a wavering voice that would have created tension even if she weren't an alarming beauty in a clingy Asian dress. But her zany smile said being introduced with a handshake was about the funniest custom ever invented, and when she laughed it seemed possible she thought the dress was only campy.

"How did you two meet?" I asked Dehlia, because she looked like she was fielding questions.

A lot of playful throat-clearing from Cody, busy at the kitchen stove.

"He overstayed his welcome," Dehlia said, as if teaching us the words.

6

"To be more accurate, I did what she was wishing I'd do. I was interviewing her before anyone knew her, six months before her Robert Johnson exhibit, and I thought, She's alone? Not anymore!"

"Exactly, Cody. That's exactly how *you* thought."

"You mean it was my job to leave? Why would I leave?"

"Yes, Cody. Why would *you* leave?" Her smile widened to a *Sheeesh* that was so dazzling it scared me into looking down.

"This was in Albuquerque," Bailey said, for my benefit.

I asked how Dehlia discovered the mythic blues man.

"From me!" Cody called from the stove. "I stole her from her rich girl life!"

"You can say that again!" Dehlia's laugh was as high as the front end of a sneeze.

I got up from my chair—so intimidated among real urban artists that the border between sitting and standing had actually been erased—and roamed with my beer to the kitchen to offer help. But Cody was already heading back. So I paused, catching my breath, taking voyeuristic notes. Their kitchen had posters of whiskery authors; my childhood home was wallpapered with candy canes, and skeleton-key themes. Through a window, the first evening lights stretched down Virgil Avenue south of Sunset, brocading a district of auto shops and warehouses, all so pretty and indifferent, still linked up by pastel flags from the '84 Olympics.

Of course, there were real families out there too, immigrants whose kids went to school with last year's backpacks, a destiny I felt worrisomely connected to, without knowing why. I lacked the self-belief of either a rich son or a poor one. But a few beers could open up a third narrative, in which all the oddness on your family tree would be vindicated, and you'd be allowed to skip all the grades you'd never passed in the school of life.

I'd chugged the rest of one beer and opened another and was back to the living room springing along as Cody was putting on a record—enacting a very ceremonial silence, for someone garrulous. The needle touched down and we heard long-distance silence, steel guitar, trembling strings.

"This is the Ry Cooder!" Bailey said. "The one Cody's writing his novel to."

Was I supposed to comment on the manuscript? Not that it wasn't good, or even great. It was a cowpoke narration that he wrote to a Ry Cooder soundtrack, and I'd kept getting lost, I don't even know if it had paragraph breaks, plus all the distractions of thinking I needed to have the right thing to say about it, and with Deliah coming in and out in her pretty vintage dress with her tinctured sigh of a voice. Bailey went another direction. "What about Elvis Wilson's profile of Cooder last week? Did you guys read it? I'm not sure I even liked it."

"You didn't," Cody assured her, and smiled. "Seriously, Elvis may be the most self-referential earthling in Los Angeles."

"Tell about that party," said Dehlia.

"Jesus! The party. Dehlia had got there late, from visiting her high school friend who had lymphoma, and Elvis—I'm not making this up—said, 'Oh, this is eerie, I was interviewing Governor Deukmejian last week and I used that very word, *lymphoma*, as a metaphor.' For real. Just Elvis being Elvis."

"Maybe that figures," Bailey said. "His interview kind of went after Ry Cooder for no reason. You know what I think, Cody? You should publish your novel's prologue as a profile of Cooder—and never mention Cooder by name! I printed it for Richard, by the way."

Cody looked pleased, but only in a supportive way, as if acknowledging some good news for Richard. "Who's editing your Valley column?" he asked me—and when I told him, he pronounced me lucky not to have so-and-so—someone who'd recently "poured rum all over himself" in an essay about the role of a Novelist. Then he looked at his watch. "I'm putting the gumbo on simmer and skateboarding to the liquor store," he said, and zipped a hoodie over his T-shirt, uncapping the last Corona. "Smokes, anyone? You need a pack of Vantages, Richard?"

"No, that's all right, thanks. Unless—I mean, if you're—"

"Smokes for Richard," he chuckled.

Dehlia's voice was tentative but urgent: "Cody, you can't. No skating with a beer."

"Au contraire. That lawyer said it's legal if it's covered."

"Which it isn't."

"Details."

"The police literally stopped him last month." Even annoyed, there was a thrill in Dehlia's eyes.

"An open-container warning," Cody said. "She makes it sound like drunk driving."

"*Ach!*" Much of her humor involved saying things in a loopy, Germanic head voice. "Would I care if you skateboarded into a *bus*? I just don't want another $60 ticket."

Cody conceded. He set his bottle beside the stereo and was gone down the stairs. We heard the clack of his wheels along the sidewalk.

———

All my sympathy for career women like Bailey came later in life. In 1985, in LA, work and play were still curled up together like bodies in a water ballet. At our first story meeting, we'd crossed Santa Monica Boulevard from a glass midrise office building to a ferny bistro where it seemed like every woman had a yellow bikini strap tied behind her neck. Bailey seemed to feel lucky to work in a bubble where fun was the point, or she was too idealistic to notice it wasn't.

I was distracted instead by the spell of Cody's girlfriend. "I should have told him to get a dessert!" she shouted, rummaging the freezer with chill air roaring out. For someone so fragile, her fingers looked very thick and hard—like a dowry of strength she might never know she had. They were fingers that could need someone to stroke them, drag a bowstring across the tendons of her sorrow.

"I absolutely won't need dessert," Bailey said. "I don't need anything at all."

Then she asked Dehlia to update us on her recent series of "white paintings" (was this an inside joke?)—and, given the floor, Dehlia turned almost comically self-serious, launching a quavering dissertation on the "theoretical and historical contextuality" of the uses of white. Her eyes looked like she was waving a flashlight across a dark, haunted cornfield.

We followed her out the kitchen door downstairs to the garage, where a dozen white canvases stood, bearing just the palest silver scribbles. One painting, Dehlia said, was of a neighbor child's knee prints in cement.

There were also some not-white paintings—spindly skeletons, African masks, Robert Johnson as the Cat in the Hat. That kind of thing was getting mainstream already, but Bailey said Dehlia got there first, only to be out-hustled by artists with braggadocio. Tying her black hair into insane artist mode, Dehlia jerked a chain to an overhead bulb—she might have been unveiling a show car, albeit half-expecting the light bulb to explode—and leaping into sight was a barn-sized canvas that after knowing her for two minutes you'd have guessed was by Dehlia.

It was an aggrieved pink so flagrant you almost had to look sideways to see it—A vagina? The grim reaper in taffeta? No: Our Lady of Guadalupe.

Bailey was busy at the knee-print painting. "And you have enough for a white show, right? Have you decided on a space?" This made Dehlia step backward, like a widow happening upon a cat burglar. "Yes—well. I might give myself a deadline for next spring. Or next fall." That was fifteen months away.

"See?" Cody was back, following our voices downstairs. "See what I'm up against with her? She hasn't done a show since New Mexico."

I had stepped close to the pink one, whose tidal strokes could make you feel you'd leaned into a spiraling vat. You could paint ten more canvases by spreading the excess off this. "Is it for sale?" I asked, and for some nearly drunk reason I thought I was making small talk. I was thinking of how show cars weren't made to sell but to shake inspiration free for other things. But Dehlia's posture changed. And I let that rise to my head while I watched Bailey stiffening in courteous surprise.

"I mean, *I'd* love to own it," I went on, trying to justify my question, but the emphasis landed wrong, until I saw that I was all the way in, as I probably wanted to be all along. Being just a little high, and very young, meant you could try on any new idea that you shouldn't, to see how it felt, and perhaps, like in chess, stay provisional, hold to safety.

"Dude!" Cody congratulated.

With a tactful, off-the-record smile, Dehlia said, "I charge $900 for paintings that size." Ringing up a sale to a new friend wasn't charity.

"It's just so good," I said, slowing down the words—and Bailey saw all of this.

The point was, Dehlia was floating now, industrious, a Cinderella seamstress shopgirl. "We'll figure out a day that works for you," she bookmarked, in a lowered tone, which both prolonged the high of the sale and pivoted us all from it.

"Did you decide to drink one skating back?" Bailey asked Cody. We were tromping upstairs to the kitchen.

"I wanted to! But I had a six-pack in each hand."

"You must be getting old," Dehlia teased.

"With that baby face?" Bailey put in. "He'll be dead before the Lucky Strikes stain his teeth."

Cody puffed smoke at us.

"It's his white-boy version of selling his soul to the devil," Dehlia said. "A cigarette."

He lifted the lid off the gumbo, handing out bowls as we assigned ourselves to the folding chairs off the kitchen. It was the first I realized they didn't actually have a table.

"For the record," Cody said, "Robert Johnson wasn't thinking so much about souls or devils. It was the actual *meaning* of a crossroads. As in, being willing to jump the next train. You should always know exactly how many steps you've drifted from the courage of the crossroads."

Bailey made a finicky face. "That feels like overthinking. Over-serious criticism."

"How about there's just a chemical truth to how someone gets that good at guitar. Not just technically good—transcendent. You see why a jealous husband might have shot him."

"Cody would rather die than be the other guy in that equation," Dehlia said, crossing her legs like an analyst.

"Exactly wrong!" Cody said, joining us with his own bowl, along with the chair he was dragging in. "I don't *never* want to die!" He had two women heckling him, and he was clearly enjoying it. "Why did Jerry West want the last shot with a basketball game on the line? He was scared of some teammate deciding his fate. Being scared is what confirms you're unafraid—I think I just proved that!"

"The head spins," Dehlia said, kneading her temples. "Maybe I should tell them the story of your knife fight."

"No one's stopping you." He reached for a cigarette with his dinner half eaten. "It's a bigger deal to you than me."

"Never believe a man who says that," said Bailey.

"Hope to die!" he said, making us all groan. "I'll just correct her when she attaches her bogus moral."

"What bogus moral exactly?" Dehlia said.

"Aren't you planning to say all wars are fought because men are little boys?"

As part of the happy audience for a war story, I worried I was pushing my luck. The memories that came up were of my dad, a ship's doctor who never saw battle in World War II, and whose street-brawling past, my mom had liked telling me, consisted of telling a rival through her sorority-house door, "I can talk to you fine from right here."

"Where do I begin?" Dehlia asked. "I was drying the dishes in Albuquerque when Cody bounded up the stairs roaring drunk with our neighbor—"

"Miguel."

"I hadn't forgotten: Miguel. And Cody was screaming, 'Give me the chopping knife! There's these guys!'"

"They took the parking space I kept for guests," Cody said. "And they were walking over toward the Rialto Theater."

"Art movie bullies!" Bailey said, joining the hilarity.

"Not to mention," Dehlia continued, "they'd gone their way. But

Miguel—who Cody worships, because he never does anything but get drunk restocking beer for the next day's party—Miguel explains that Cody had promised to slash their tires, and they threatened to find him if he did."

Cody shrugged.

"And suddenly I'm reasoning on his level! I'm saying, 'Cody, sweetheart, you know I would never deny you a sharp implement the moment you asked, but—"

"Were you laughing?" I asked.

"Well, Cody was. But he also could have been about to cry," she teased. "He downed a beer and started searching through the knife drawer and then he and Miguel went tearing down the stairs and you could hear ... voices. And possibly giggling, as they're possibly gutting a tire. But branches are blocking my view and it's a very dark night. Then Miguel says, very concerned, in a stage whisper: 'I don't know—I think their car was gray!'"

"Oh, no," Bailey said.

"Eventually the strangers came back with a bag from the liquor store—apparently they weren't going to the Rialto at all—laughing so hard they were practically peeing, because guess what? Cody slashed the wrong car's tires."

"Don't leave out the good part," Cody said amiably.

"Yes, Cody ran at one of them, and all I knew was I had to call 911, because that's what a grownup does—" She socked Cody on the knee. "But I hesitated, worrying he'd be the one who'd get arrested."

"Oh," Cody said, "I remember Miguel's moment now. He looked like he'd suddenly forgotten to be drunk, and he shouted, *'I'll get Arnulfo!—wait, Arnulfo's in prison.'*"

"I never tire of that line."

"Tell what happened to the other guys," Cody said.

"Yes, this is the epilogue Cody hopes you'll remember. He held them off three times from getting into their car until finally the police got him to lay off."

"Cody didn't get arrested?" I asked. "Even after slashing the tire?"

"Guess whose car it was," Dehlia said, unsmiling.

13

Bailey and I were speechless.

"I made him buy me *four* new tires."

"The moral is don't fuck with me," Cody said.

"The moral is it cost you four new tires." A pause. "You're not going to correct me?"

"Why? You got off more than I did, afterwards."

"OOOOh Cody," she pretended, and kissed him sloppily on the neck.

"Don't make fun if you're making fun of yourself!" He banged a drum solo on his knees.

"You're drunk again," was all she could say.

Cody curtsied and Dehlia's face composed itself like the face of a boxer who is taking the count. Now Cody seemed sympathetic. He touched the back of her hair, and I thought he might have been pushing, downward, with pressure. But when I looked closer, he was stroking her neck. "I go too far. She's right. Why do you get into it with me? I go too far, and I'm sorry." He gathered a couple of empty bowls. "Notice who does the cooking *and* the dishes?"

———

Bailey asked if I had a near-death story too. It fell to her to moderate the conversation, I guess, and the obviousness of doing it made her look like she was the host when she was only trying to help.

I was afraid mine was going to end more like a poem than an adventure. Once, my friend Scott and I took a speedboat along the rim of Lake Powell, in Utah, which has 2,000 miles of continuous shoreline. Somewhere shaded by cliffs, we drifted with the current a long time into a winding fractal with canyon walls that rose straight up. As far in as there was, we killed the motor, reveling in the quiet pool of our arrival. Half hideaway, half dungeon. Gently the boat bobbed and rocked. Only Scott couldn't restart the motor. We tried and tried. We exhausted ourselves failing to row our way out. We blew our emergency whistles till our faces ached and it was getting dark and the temperature dropped like lead. Eventually, for no reason at all, we got the motor to start.

That was all. I tried to stretch the story out with jokes about cannibalism (*"Who really wins?"*). But what I wished I could have pondered out loud, more likely alone with Bailey, was how the prospect of death felt more like an absence than a presence. How the sky looked exactly as inviting as ever but farther away, because you'd done something unforgivably stupid, and the sky was no longer yours. There Scott and I had sat, like both of our lovers had left us. With the whole smarter, happier world on the other side of its sandstone partition.

Anyway, no one at Cody's seemed to expect any such confession from me, and my turn passed to Bailey. Who, as I've said, would have accepted me no matter what story I told.

Seriously: Why did we survive? It was like we'd been chosen for life, but not in a flattering way. Of course, there are no explanations in this lifetime for who escapes, or postpones, bad luck. In the Bible, I think, God told Job something like that. Although, even there, the Bible was obliged to offer a back story: a bet with the devil, from which the Lord, gambler that he was, like Robert Johnson, could not back down.

These days I think that the instinct to survive shows up, strangely familiar, when we find ourselves in need of it. Had the boat's motor not restarted, perhaps I would have paddled, then dropped anchor for a time to gather strength, then paddled ten feet more, and on and on, until we were in whistle range. But I had no access to such experience back then. So the way Scott and I got out was by luck, by entitlement—I rode on the back of my friend's certainty that the lake was ours. He piloted us back to the docks by moonlight, soaring over whitecaps.

―――――――

The real reason I'm writing about Bailey, all these years later, is that my 27-year-old son, Philip, asks me to.

He hasn't experienced an exciting young adulthood himself, despite running away from psychiatric hospitalization one summer to demand the universe give him one, that time winding up on the

15

streets. He also has the idea that the music and art scene of LA in the 1980s was special, more egalitarian and open to sensitive souls than today, and that Bailey, whom I've talked about so often, was the image of those times.

"Your generation had it all," he used to say, with genuine admiration. Later, when his illness made him surly, he'd add: *"Didn't you."*

He even got to meet Bailey—once at Farmers' Market when he was two years old, and then again at eighteen, at her apartment, on the very eve of his first mental break. She turned him on to CDs by The Czars and by Gang of Four, and he sank back on one of her chairs, feeling the same no-fault ease I had felt there years before. She was in her sixties then, heavy as ever, and when we left, he volunteered that he thought she was cute.

Sometimes I think that all along, when I was clinging with such weird, vicarious self-regard to what felt special about coming alive in the 1980s, I was trying to pilfer a taste of it for this future son.

Housesitting in what was starting to be Koreatown. I lay around like a Zen master with my flip flops beneath a wood frame bed. Through some white steel security screens, you could see vines and dirt, practically taste the beauty of neglect.

San Francisco on a rare hot day. The yuppies would emerge from hibernation with their ice chests to visit Golden Gate beach. The water would be cold enough to bend bones, and the men wore plaid swimming trunks in homage to their Cold War fathers.

I know that many of these treasures seem shortsighted looking back, when so much hardship, both here and abroad, was going on at the very same time. But when you're young, and death is just a topic swirled in a glass, ignorance makes an almost moral argument for itself. Why not savor all the comfort that you can?

To still see ignorant comfort as an open night sky instead of just a canvas one—maybe that's a stage of history that Americans are seeing pass. Maybe it resides in another part of the world, now, or maybe it's for new families arriving here, that same sense of openness that I used to feel growing up when I did.

The thing is, I've watched my son idealize this past, maybe even harder than I did—this idea of a better, more welcoming birthplace that he wasn't born in time to see, with Bailey Kavanagh the very center of it—and it all feels almost more alive to me for his having missed it.

———

The only way Bailey was going to tell a near-death story was to make it about someone else's near death, and apologize for not knowing how to make sense of it. And she was beautiful doing that. Which I know sounds like I was in love with her—I wasn't. But right then and there, I wanted her terribly. I wanted one more chance with her in bed.

She was looking straight at Dehlia, as if her story was just for women, and I felt a pang of doom as it occurred to me that buying Dehlia's pink painting meant hanging it up in my little apartment.

A girl in Japan, Bailey said, went high-diving on the Army base without a swim cap. Either the girl's onyx hair got inhaled by the suction of the pool's drain, or its weight jerked back on entry, snapping her neck. Whichever version Bailey really told means I must have made the other one up. But I do remember she envied that hair intensely. *It swirled even when dry*, Bailey said. And the fact that the girl was so otherworldly made her perfect to be brooded over by someone like Bailey. So she kept asking questions that took us away from the story. *How do divers know where to turn in midair? Is beauty a kind of talent?*

But the one detail she could not remember was the crucial one: *Had the long-haired diver died?*

Did you recall blood? we kept asking. *Blue lips? CPR?*

Bailey just shook her head.

"She was exactly your type of gorgeous!" she told Dehlia. "No, I'd remember if she died." She steadied her hand against Dehlia's arm, as if promising not to laugh. "I'm sure of it now. She only got her neck broken."

Dehlia's eyes looked like she might run off and cry, or else she was just bewildered—soon Bailey herself was laughing, as if at her own

17

clumsiness. "All I've ever wanted was to be gorgeous like you," she assured Dehlia, reaching for some meritorious pain.

———————

At home, I wrote a humor piece for the *LA Weekly* inspired by the concept of time-sharing another man's girlfriend. It was in the cringey voice of a guy who'd anticipated a little pushback and had thought through his counterarguments, negotiating for stolen moments, a few prolonged kneeling hugs. It was funny. It got printed.

No one brought up the sale of the painting right away, and it would have been awkward for Dehlia to remind me. But Bailey and I brought her with us to a show at Club Lingerie while Cody was on deadline, and there we were, the three of us.

Afterward I drove Bailey home first. I had made a monastic show of not drinking, and with the motor running, I offered to walk her to her door, but she declined. From how polite I must have seemed to Dehlia, I think anyone could see what was shaping up.

When we reached Dehlia's, I said, "I can walk you up," in a tone of tragic respect. I turned the ignition off.

"Don't be silly," she said, "I'd have you up but Cody's turned off the lights."

"Well," I said, "Bailey has really nice friends."

Jasmine all around, we performed one of her hilarious handshakes.

But now, with each one's neediness locating the other's, like pilgrims to an ancestral monument, it was delivery day for the canvas. I played assistant and Dehlia worked, unroping the hatchback of her car while I credibly inspected the knots. Inside my unit, I almost got annoyed at her for not helping arrange where the painting should go. She only leaned it someplace stable, acting overtly absorbed in that act.

As I leaned in to kiss her, she gave a nervous, questioning giggle but she never moved.

Making out was an opera of mmms and ahhs, pulling away to ensure this was okay, realizing it was less awkward to kiss some more. I did not want to go farther yet than kissing. I hadn't planned that far ahead. So I whispered, "Again, soon," and we walked to her car in the kind of stupor that meant everything then.

Back upstairs, though, the painting's pink glare filled my small room like an illness. I even reentered twice, looking for an offhand view, trying to catch my apartment through the eyes of someone else entering. Why hadn't she talked me out of this? Certainly, art involved danger, but did that mean I should build the only room of my home around it? She might as well have left me a newborn.

But to give back the painting implied I was an art coward, and that I would never be Dehlia's equal, or Cody's. I resolved to get used to the painting. Frame its shockingness as a kind of adventure. And this plan got me as far as the next afternoon. Then I just gave up.

So we decided on the phone I could swap the picture out for one of her African-mask ones, and Dehlia didn't seem in any hurry to judge me. In fact, she sounded loopy again, freed from all care—with that high, Germanic laugh that said we were all just kids, playacting romance.

We spent a Christmas at her mom and stepdad's ranch house in Escondido. The country setting could have been paradise, except that the mother's every offstage question to Dehlia sounded so worried, you'd think her daughter's beauty was going to fade within the week. By then I'd learned that Dehlia's biological father was a suicide, and that the best thing Dehlia ever painted (a portrait of Nat King Cole) she subsequently blackened one awful night by trying to perfect it. The stepfather sat in a recliner, while Dehlia's mom busied herself in that sentence-serving way of second wives. She'd landed in picturesque safety, determined to pull Dehlia aboard. But she could not make her lifeboat look like life.

Maybe I was a symbol of hope to those parents. Once, through their kitchen window, they'd seen Cody bully Dehlia in their driveway—not with fists, but scaring them that he might, shoving her along to the car when she was jammed between staying or going.

———

Months before, during his late innings with Dehlia, Cody had taken me on jaunts to record stores, trading in review CDs for old jazz finds, several of which he gifted me, as a sign of his largesse. After their final quarrel, he came over to complain, pacing my bedroom floor (Dehlia's African painting and all).

Had he no other male friends? To say the least, I saw both their sides.

But I'd always known, like a reporter, to keep thoughts like that to myself. He said he found his hand-held tape recorder smashed to pieces after what would be their last argument. He'd confronted Dehlia in calm disbelief: "Did you do this?"—one of those small, obvious questions that makes clear it means the world. Dehlia had denied it. And only my agreeing with Cody that this made no sense at all could console him. Something in me had always dreamed, maybe known, that my patient, brooding nature could also be my strength. Although I sensed I might never be the kind of winner whose win comes first.

I neither condemned nor excused Cody. I thought of him brandishing that broken tape recorder, and I thought of Dehlia's pride and shame at having broken it, and what I saw was their raw desperation for each other. To me, back then, that was great love. It gave Dehlia and me its long shadow, like the legend of an earlier generation.

The day after dinner at Cody's, when Bailey phoned to ask if I'd enjoyed myself, I broke into a sweat and withheld from her the course I'd set myself on. She did not press, nor did she act extremely hurt when I started seeing Dehlia. Except in whatever artist way Bailey always seemed hurt, and wanting to explore whatever the mystery was of being people young and hurting. It could even be viewed as uncaring, her letting me blunder after Dehlia if I would. She sent me tapes of songs, and letters in her chunky cursive, and still I almost never thought of Bailey, except on the occasions when I'd write for her.

Zealots: 1983

———◆———

WHEN HE GOT HIMSELF hired as executive editor of a groovy West Coast magazine, it was becoming possible for a reporter like Jim Warren, with Western Washington Press Club trophies clanking in the back of his car, to picture Hollywood success. There were writers from *Texas Monthly* and *New York Magazine*, barely middle-aged, who wrote screenplays left-handed but magazine features with all their hearts, and then retired onto beaches in Jamaica. You'd see them in contributor's photos, the boy-wonder haircuts, the billowing JFK swim trunks that proclaimed their escape. Even in the years just after Watergate, this was a pretty lofty self-image for magazine writers to entertain. But like a lot of new ideas in the 1970s, it felt more like an earthy timeless one that had never been given a proper trial.

I first shook Warren's hand—twice, before he could stop us—back when Bailey Kavanagh had me in for my first real editorial lunch. But I knew all about his voice in print, had been breathing that in like cedar wood, cedar with flecks of pot: that whole mix of Ivy League stature and hippie cool that converted me to buying wool slacks and penny loafers that day, making me look like a job-seeker from guidance class.

He was tall: former-basketball-player tall, with a melancholy way of seeming more by flaunting less, which let you know he didn't grow up in LA. Even though people like him were always the ones running things in LA.

Then he left the lobby and I could relax, nursing Bailey's alleged crush on my writing. (I actually had a girlfriend, in Boston—an art student who'd picked me out on a trip west, as if for a musical she was casting about a loud Boston girl, forever being cat-called by jerks, who finally spots a boy timid enough for her to trust.)

Warren got his job by writing an application letter that became legendary because they hired him by printing it—one of those Hail Mary shots that, in the highlight reel of history, turns out to be a sure thing every time you play it back. It blended Hemingway's grace, Will Rogers' drawl, and all the just-right local bona fides, like his use of the phrase "bene gesserit" to describe the Dodgers' princely owner Peter O'Malley. Once, I'd taped a lead of his to my bathroom mirror.

I'm a writer, not a dune buggyist. My brother-in-law is a dune-buggyist, not a writer. Between the two of us, however, we just might have a story.

Even the looming darkness explored by Warren's magazine—the Quaalude-peddling teens, the child-molesting teachers, the Sacramento street preacher turning cult figure—never seriously threatened the vibe of breezy decompression that his whole generation seemed to be enjoying together in the pages of every issue—an information-delivery ritual so basic to grownup civilization, you couldn't imagine it ever passing away.

But I was a wannabe punk in 1983, afraid that even the other black sheep saw through me. At my older sister's complex in Culver City, with the gas barbecues and coin-op Jacuzzis, I filled notepads with seditious verse, finding alchemy in words like "varve" and "melanoma" and "dismay." In bars, I stood paralyzed by the jukebox (would my musical choice be some biker's last straw?)—flipping the song menu for an anthem that would both offend my baffled father and make him take me in his arms.

Picture Warren sliding into his wife's car upon arriving to LAX.

The bus benches say "LA's the Place," but plainly it isn't, yet. It is the Sun Belt, giddy and unbeholden. The horizon feels like an arena of adoring fans, begging him to shoot. The Hamburger Hamlet in Brentwood is filled with golden women: screenwriters who'd been too odd or too smart in college. At the Post Office, his neighbors practically drink daiquiris in line. He has to struggle not to look ten years ahead, to the kids skateboarding in the Palisades, to the dinner guests reframing the meaning of middle age at every milestone birthday.

One morning, paired up in Bailey's cubicle, he looms over the next issue's cover art.

"I don't mind 'The Masque after Hours,'" he says. "But why does the photo make the very same point? We need an emblem, a phone on a nightstand—"

"Oh, I think I love that!"

It takes a moment for Warren to remember that Bailey feels no conflict about applauding an interesting idea prior to understanding it.

"And the cover line could be a mock public-service ad. *It's 4 a.m. Shall we tell you where your kids are?*"

He watches her nodding, shrewdly at first—then sublimely, with all her being. She is artsy, tipping toward fat, with turquoise eyes to go with the finger-gelled blue spikes in her hair. If it were Bailey's magazine, the cover line would address the kids, not the parents. There would be a payphone by an overflowing john.

"Ooh, it's perfect," she moans. "It seems wrong not to close shop!"

It's 1 p.m., and Warren is the slightest bit afraid she really means this.

He ventures on, reading from a narrow spiral pad. "Now, for the Christmas Memories feature. Everyone seems to like 'Five writers writing and a partridge in a palm tree.' But should it be seven writers? Nine?" Inviting her in—it's understood that he knows fewer California writers than she does.

———————

Or was I living in Beachwood Canyon then? No, still Culver City, proofreading children's schoolbooks—but my plan was to live on

23

Beachwood Drive, if only at the base of it, in a brownstone with fire escapes and dank walkways. I resented my older sister's singles complex because of its whole lack of *varve*. And for two years before that, I resented San Francisco.

Why had I ever left LA?

In letters to editors, I had criticized the San Francisco cast of an LA play. And the distance of the BART station from my flat. I lay daily under a sunlamp clipped to my bookshelf.

My father had flown to town and met me at a restaurant in the Marina, where he picked up a woman closer to my age than his.

Pride of his immigrant parents, a ship's doctor in WWII, he had progressed to silk suits, then season tickets to the Lakers and Rams. He held his parenting discussions from behind a desk. Each house he bought was farther west, the auburn lights outside his living-room window a *Tonight Show* backdrop. What did his story leave my generation to become? You can be orphaned by being born where people are supposed to dream of arriving.

The first thing I ever sent Warren's magazine was my unsolicited "I Lost My Heart In San Francisco" essay—a brave, incantatory work! I'd thought—and did Warren even read its hypnotic ending? Where the zombie punk girl marches implacably up Market Street, "her song rising hymn-like, against odds that were becoming, with each moment, more apparent"?

"I could have quit over them not wanting it," Bailey told me by phone.

Then, before hanging up, she tacked something on about a special Christmas edition in the works. "Personal memories. The kind of thing you'd probably be good at."

Had Bailey just given me an assignment? Anxiety makes you a terrible listener.

Once, when I was in college, a visiting speaker who practiced Tai Chi kicked off an experimental dance demonstration with the words: "Would the volunteers join me onstage?" The operative word was *the*, *the* volunteers. But I'd been chatting with a classmate and only halfway heard.

24

I climbed onto the auditorium stage. Somewhere, the rest of the volunteers had obtained robes. A bit of recorded Eastern music began to play, and the other dancers' bodies—followed by mine, in a troubling delay—pantomimed catching masses of celestial energy like medicine balls, then pushing this energy outward again, to the audience, to the universe. As a group, almost, we began to revolve, pirouetting on alternating feet, only one of us stumbling, while from the audience my friend covered his eyes.

I could think of no way to tell Bailey I hadn't been listening. And if I did write a true Christmas memory of my own—the one about living in the Valley and asking a Christmas charity for a Buick Riviera—it would be both too much in the real spirit of Christmas and not enough. It would violate the benign, eccentric groove of Jim Warren's *West Coast* magazine. My story would have no stoned alumni of The Farm attempting to roast turkey. Or dog races in Tijuana. Or Santas on surfboards.

Within minutes, though, I was spared from deciding. Bailey called once more, this time to say they had decided to use big-name writers only—which both confirmed my exciting news and destroyed it. I thanked her for letting me know. I felt sad, but also, shamefully, relieved.

I stumbled downstairs, practically falling out of the building into a San Francisco Sunday. Sea air fluttered like a pennant. The bars were strung like charms along every avenue, and the time of day was whatever was left in the fourth quarter of a 49ers game. On Divisadero, I passed a beautiful home that once had rejected me as a boarder. It belonged to a dowager whose voice had smiled on the phone but not when I arrived, and I stopped there, subjecting myself to the shame, wondering if salvation might lie just the other side of pure forlornness. I had no money to enter a bar, another wrong that was pregnant to be made right, and I envied the drinkers for not having to write magazine stories on a Sunday afternoon. Which I suddenly realized was what I needed to do.

I'm not taking credit for this realization—it was more like insisting that my future come choose me. Like when Tony in *West Side*

Story takes to the streets screaming for Chino to come shoot him, too. So, the next morning, when the great columnist Herb Caen inexplicably backed out, as if I'd always known he would, Bailey bought my Buick Riviera story, and how could she not, with opening lines that were pure Jim Warren:

> *In December 1966, plenty of things were happening to people who did not live in the San Fernando Valley. Those need not concern anyone.*

———————

Another smart young person was rounded up for lunch, a photo editor wearing black cat whiskers she'd scraped up, bizarrely, from a fashion shoot. "What do people even order, martinis?" she asked at our crossing light.

"Make sure we spend a minute talking about your piece," Bailey said, poking me. The noon sun beat down.

"Let me pick your brains, the both of you," the photo editor said, and pulled a glossy eight-by-eleven from her large purse. "For Date-liners." In the photo, a female artist posed beside her latest work, a pyramid constructed entirely of Alan Alda head shots. "What kind of text should it get? A mini-essay?"

Bailey's face lit up and she said I ought to write this too. Then the light turned green, and she put her arm inside mine, as though we were already drunk, while the whiskered photo editor linked my other one, making me Dorothy of Oz.

So while the nation watched M*A*S*H* on CBS that night, I was deconstructing it, praising the sitcom star's winning grin but simultaneously daring to ridicule him. For perhaps the first time, the show's opening theme song, "Suicide is Painless," fluttered like the rerun it would become.

Whatever awful thing I wrote, Bailey Kavanagh raved about. She took her mascot-genius status to another local magazine and then another, somehow pushing all my odd, LA-native takes past her

26

superiors. I taught her about the healing properties of Vin Scully's voice. I pitched my crushes on other women as feature essays.

When a celebrated old-school detective lapsed into a drunken, racist anecdote, I quoted him gleefully, in full.

She'd fallen in love with LA as a child from DC, and my stories, she said, reawakened that de Tocqueville state. We'd go for drives disguised as lunches, and I'd make up alternate histories of the ghostly neighborhoods. For one essay, we looked for the birthplace of the Beatles' "Rubber Soul," that Motherland past the next range of hills, where lovers went off to sleep in the bath.

But there had to be times I nearly wrecked things. When one of my stories used made-up book titles in describing an interview subject's shelf—I had planned to check the real titles in my notes, then forgot—Bailey's rebuke was so furious that I saw at once how generous her hazy allegiance had been.

Absolutely none of this, of course, could succeed with Jim Warren. He turned down anything I sent him. So many months passed that I more or less gave up trying. Until, during a brutal September heat wave, I sat pining for the lunch truck at that educational publisher in Culver City, proofreading schoolbooks so watered-down that even the first-graders could smell censorship, and a voice in my head announced: *Between the two of us, we just may have a story.*

It is said that good news never arrives by mail. But in Jim Warren's era, it did, on crisp West Coast letterhead.

Dear Richard, I am forwarding your proposal about the sorry state of schoolbook publishing to Ben Boly with my recommendation for feature treatment. The Big Brothering of our language and literature by pressure groups of the left and right has concerned me for some time. The angle you suggest is an excellent one—it makes us fighting mad.

Fighting mad, Jim Warren said! My proposal had made Jim Warren feel such things.

———————

I did my job, or I pretended to. But my whole body kept telling me I was doomed.

I flew to a state textbook conference in Sacramento. I shook hands with the reformist State Superintendent of Schools. I interviewed school librarians, wishing I could ask stupid, David Letterman-style questions about whether real librarians practiced shaking out their hair.

A congressman from Orange County, I'd once read, stopped making love to his wife after the Gulf of Tonkin attack, informing her *there was a war on.* He was ridiculed, as the over-serious are, but didn't he deserve our admiration too?

At the worst possible moment in deadline week, Sylvie, my Boston girlfriend, flew out for two days, hinting of moving west for good. Teasing her Worcester accent, my buddy Wren got her laughing on the phone about me having to "Woak, woak, woak," and the two must have giggled for seven minutes before I bounced my electric typewriter across the floor.

It wasn't just the pressure of impersonating one of Jim Warren's A-list reporters. It wasn't just abstaining from alcohol till the story was completed. With this manuscript, I was offering Warren my soul. I wove in sad soliloquys about the spirit-crushing American workplace. Deadpan vignettes from editorial meetings in which I, as Warren's eyes and ears, beheld the gang-rape of our literary heritage. I followed the life cycle of a children's book that was meant to include a near-drowning adventure, but had been revised to give the characters water wings. "We strapped water wings on the children," I'd written, "when literature would no longer do."

For more than two weeks, Warren did not reply.

"Richard," said Wren on our next hike, his arms swinging wide, "you know I like your writing. But I'm not following this manuscript at all."

Warren's editorial notes arrived in the next day's mail.

Dear Richard,

    Educational publishing is one heck of an interesting subject. Your proposal is worthy of 60 Minutes—perhaps you have that proposal nearby?

    Let me apologize, first, for not having framed the following question at an earlier stage. But what kind of story does this aim to be, precisely? A confessional? An expose? Magical realism? Right now it's a little of each, and I'm not certain that the weave fully works. Not to suggest you should throw out every scene—a couple are brilliant. But I find myself wondering if your story may need (ironic, given the subject at hand) to be dumbed down for a general audience.

    Suppose we were to begin at the beginning. There's a problem with educational publishing. The issue is lousy textbooks. California as bellwether of the nation. (You have facts and figures on page 17 that belong in your nut graf.) Enter Superintendent Silverman. He is your newspeg. That textbook conference in Sacramento offers us an insider's view of an important political player in action. Yet you veer instead to a lurid dream sequence involving a librarian behind that lunch truck in Culver City.

Two full pages later:

I know this all might sound discouraging, but Harold, our intern from Loyola Marymount, is a very accomplished line editor. His perceptions can be quite valuable to a struggling writer. Assuming you take his notes to heart and pull this together in a few weeks' time—I'm confident you can— we'd like to explore a few interesting art possibilities.

This was my cue, in other words—to be a pro, to do my time in the Italian summer leagues of journalism. To pass through a perfectly challenging, but perfectly finite, series of character tests before receiving an I-never-doubted-you embrace from the immaculate and unknowable Jim Warren. Instead, each rewrite was more grandiose than the last, more tortured yet hopeful, and each response from

Warren more disappointing. "Sorry I suggested that tack. . . Better move that paragraph back where it was. . . I should have flagged this back in Draft #2, but you fooled us with your pleasing rhetoric."

Trudging the sidewalk, my song rising hymn-like, I fell into Ports bar and found company, a handful of slovenly writers. Wren waved me to their corner booth. Beside him was Dean Temkin, the bogusly urbane reporter for a Marxist radio network. There was the Echo Park poetess in a muumuu, and her husband, the bushy author of a monograph on West Coast utopianism.

"Unionizing writers is worse than herding kittens," Temkin said.

A novelist with British supergroup hair declared, "Writers don't join groups. A writer has to feel unbound."

"Unbound," Wren laughed. "Like a pamphlet?"

"Like a herd of kittens," the poet said.

"Richard, sit down," said Dean Temkin. "How does it feel to know that Jim Warren is assigning eight pieces for every one he accepts? They can afford to because of the criminally low kill fees."

These were turning out to be not the worst people to postpone productive grief with, and after three or four boilermakers—at last I could drink—and some gossip that had no connection to the business of Hollywood except that we lived there, it emerged how I might help them. I could serve as the first local delegate to the American Freelance Writers Union convention in New York, then report home to make a quick, informational speech at a recruiting event.

"I cannot do that," I vowed —it was the speech I was thinking of—but they took me for trying to sound gracious.

Within days, they'd bought me a ticket. A YA author from the Westchester, NY, delegation would give me a guest bedroom. Sylvie would rent a car and meet me after the closing session to drive to her sister's in Worcester, MA. Wearing suede boots that she'd given me for my birthday, I boarded a redeye flight, its aisles jammed with investment bankers in loosened ties, and found myself in a lecture hall at SUNY: acoustic panels, theater chairs, just like out west, just like in experimental-music class, but on the complete other side of the continent—could the mind even hold such a paradox?

When it was time to deliver greetings from the new Los Angeles chapter, I fumbled, "Well, we got me here!"—reddening even before the sentence was out. There seemed no way in English to arrange the words.

I sat down, roughed up my hair with one hand, and a gavel struck for lunch.

Behind me, two voices hovered. They were a pale sex columnist for the *Long Island Weekly*, along with a gay poet who was even paler. The Brooklyn delegation.

"So when *you got you here*," Devorah Miller said, "Barry elbowed me, and we shot each other the question."

"The question?"

"'Are you going to sleep with him, or should I?'"

With a bread knife that Devorah Miller had used to lift some spilled candle wax, I was deepening a groove in the beveled edge of her wooden nightstand. Devorah noticed this but appeared only idly curious. "Are you okay?"

"Oh, sure. I don't know."

I was counting my new treasures: I was a jet traveler, a national delegate to a writers' convention. I had slept with the kind of New York woman who wore glasses in bed and typed in her panties.

Devorah pulled me by the shoulder, and we had a bumpy, childish kiss, the kind that made you want to go back and improve it.

"All right," she said, getting up. "Because I thought we had a relatively good start. For people just learning each other's bodies."

She started filling a bathtub, which was in the kitchen, beyond a counter landslid by manuscripts, and what a cave the apartment was. A front stoop with planters stood outside. In Brooklyn, the only rebellion available was by closing the blinds.

When she'd decanted unequal parts cold and boiling water, she plunked herself in, a pink dumpling—hair frizzing, nipples swollen. "Do you want in?"

Just that word, *in*.

"My girlfriend is going to pick me up after today's session," I said. "My girlfriend, Sylvie."

Devorah began massaging her nipples, then slid her hands down, alternating thumbs beneath the suds. Her back began to arch. "Is this going to be—a problem?"

"No, it's not. I just—I haven't thought it through." I came over and gave her a kiss but stopped myself, said sorry. Then kissed her again.

Devorah found this spectacle weird but amusing, between her mounting grimaces. Then I stood quiet and transfixed while she finished herself off before opening her arms wide toward me.

I said, "I probably still need to wake up all the way."

My weight was leaning more toward the tub than away, though. So I went ahead and climbed in. The more wrong everything felt, the more fitting, as if I'd found the missing ending to my story for Jim Warren.

That afternoon, when Sylvie met me at the convention, Devorah shouted in a sisterly way: "He's a little sore, but no worse for wear!"

My boot heels squeaked, and a little collective gasp spread through the corridor, which I may have made worse by trying to smile good-bye to my fellow delegates.

Why did Sylvie forgive me? It is astonishing what a drinking girl-friend takes in stride. Once having mistaken your defect as the thing that makes you worthy of her love. All the way to Boston in a light rain, we shared a bottle of something, a champagne she'd planned to surprise me with, and I think her mood was similar to mine: a vag-abond feeling, a chance to imagine yourself in a foreign movie about compromised relationships, and I knew that our problem would keep us up talking into the morning hours, on her ragged couch as we held hands and tasted and discarded the option of breaking up.

And even so, I let Devorah stay in my Beachwood apartment during a union trip west. I met her at baggage claim and drove her ten miles out of my way without saying so, just to show off, as if acci-dentally, the new downtown skyline, the upstart highrises, spaced like fence posts. "Aren't we kind of doubling back?" she asked.

"No. It only seems that way."

Somehow I was loyal to Sylvie that night, but Devorah was canny. Over morning coffee, it unfolded she'd been a mistress of Jim Warren's boss, Ben Boly—a man who, unforgivably, ridiculed her sex column at a dinner party. I told her how Warren had tormented me, and she beckoned me close, enacting a hug of deep solidarity. Then she guided my head down, unsnapped her jeans and began to move me, as if applying makeup. The whole world smelled like old denim and unpaid bills, and I could imagine saying that I loved her.

Devorah, I'm sure, didn't share my sense of gravity. She had me drive her to the home of a public radio correspondent she knew, and I watched the two of them conceive and compose a hit piece for afternoon drive-time about "*West Coast Magazine*'s War on Writers," with several sentences devoted entirely to Jim Warren.

A handful of phone calls, sources on record—this was how the big brains did it.

Devorah Miller's story was credited with hastening, perhaps even causing, Ben Boly's decision to give the middle finger to Los Angeles and leave. Jim Warren's exit was less dramatic, at once courtly and bittersweet. In his colorful life he'd been a journeyman reporter, a shoe salesman with a Ph.D., a strong forward in basketball; he would land on his feet. Solar gardening called him now. Professorships. Books.

"I'm thinking of killing the story, though," Devorah teased when we got back to the tar beach rooftop of my apartment. "Should I kill the story?" She'd stepped out of her jeans again and was waving the loose pages behind her head while I grasped for them.

———————

A long time after this—my 27-year-old son, Philip, would have just turned three—we visited San Francisco as father-son tourists. I was newly divorced from his mom, Nola (a proofreader, but you might remember her tottering through some B movies of the seventies, always someone's attention-starved kid sister), and as I carried him outside from a meal out with friends, he fell heavily asleep over my shoulder.

That's when I realized where we were. It was that spot, or close enough: the place where I'd lucked onto the idea to go ahead and write a Christmas story for Bailey Kavanagh. Where the dowager lived who'd seen something wrong with me.

I paused, at least until Philip's weight started to really crush me—thinking, I suppose, about where the molecules that became the DNA that became the son on my shoulder had been distributed when I was young in San Francisco. Thinking about the chances and choices that had wind-blown our future realities to here. But if the location held any special sacredness, you wouldn't have known it tonight. Only damp sidewalk and foghorn, the full-bodiedness of a San Francisco night.

This is the son who, at eighteen, was diagnosed with a disabling mental illness. TV commercials spoke to him in code, random motorists made shoot-yourself gestures. All his life before then—you hear this often enough from parents to make you superstitious—he'd just been special. At the Halloween parade, you'd be forgiven for noticing mainly him, lowering his ghost mask over and over to see how you liked him.

I once read that a firstborn child with hardship is considered by some to be a mark of blessing, of God's unusual trust. There are even days when I'm receptive to this view—days spent helping him build a stable life—the sorting of meds, the standing in line for his weekly bloodwork. The whole seasons when he'll seem close to mastering an enemy that no one really ever masters.

On other days, though, I'm prone to daydream. What if a guardian angel were assigned to my case? What if Sylvie, or more likely Bailey, were to locate me now, after so many years, caregiver baggage and all?

But their crushes on me required that I be a young, wannabe writer, desperately insecure, a creature of pure potential, and always dreaming of something farther off. Not to say this is a less necessary form of love.

Jim Warren, as the sort of journalists I've lost touch with know, died in the nineties—not on any palmy island, but in Orleans, Massachusetts. According to his obituary, which I've looked up long after the fact, he wrote two very well-reviewed books (one exposing a suicide cult, the other about a vintner in Sebastopol who murdered a labor organizer). Both were optioned to Hollywood, though Jim Warren never saw them produced. A daughter, however, was taking up the cause of the latter project, which at last report was in production at Universal. A *New York Times* profile showed her, the daughter—who'd developed an Amazon Original miniseries, the caption said—seated bare-shouldered on a patio in what had to have been Italy, beside a wooden table that was six inches thick.

———————

The same day West Coast published Jim Warren's resignation letter—likening this state to a "vast and visionary pitch meeting for the future" in which "each generation gets one chance to score"—Wren was landing Sylvie a maid's quarters at the top of Beachwood Canyon.

"Suppose we take a little drive," was how Wren led off on the phone—what was he, from homicide?

His phone call caught us reading rental ads, close to fighting over why I wouldn't let her move into my studio open-ended, so I was pretty relieved, basically. I was celebrating with a few beers at sundown when Wren drove up, ridiculously, in an Austin Healy 3000 BJ8.

"Don't ask how I do these things. I just do."

"Fucking shit!" Sylvie whacked his arm. "Where am I?" We jack-knifed ourselves into the back seat.

"I won't even ask why I'm here," Bailey said, leaning across the front. "And this is Sylvie, from Worcester? You're so beautiful!"

"Bailey is Wren's editor, too," I explained.

I was having what amounted to my very favorite experience of youth: the sense that you're living as yourself and vicariously both at once. I had an extra six pack at my feet, and between Sylvie and me sat the magazine, whose pages I'd caressed as much as read.

35

"So, to be clear—this is that friend's car that you wanted to write about?" Bailey asked Wren. "With the parts all over the driveway?"

"Leftover car parts aren't a good sign," I said.

"You remember Clive, Richard," Wren said, shifting gears. "The guy who did the old Hoover commission documentary. He bought this with the royalties."

"And he let you take it out?" Sylvie said, eyes wide.

Wren was gleeful. "Oh, Miss Beantown. A night like this is legal grounds."

I inhaled the dank, gravedigger essence of the hillside, foresty and mysterious while never taking you more than walking distance from a laundromat or a bus. There were hollows and burrows and hairpin twists, and the foliage on narrow streets pushed so close it triggered Bailey's allergies. Her eyes teared up so badly she could not see.

"It's like with binoculars. I have never seen a thing through binoculars. Which way is the Hollywood sign?"

"Well, we're above the Scientology spire," Wren said. "And the mountains are behind you." We spun hard. "They're kind of circling you now."

"That really tells me nothing," Bailey said.

"There are zeppelins, hovering," I said. "Jeeps bouncing by, after a war."

"Totally!" she applauded, still weeping.

At the summit—really there was no lot higher—the home perched like one of those pristine canyon synagogues surrounding LA. A real synagogue might honestly be smaller.

It belonged to the Konigs, a couple Wren's parents had known since law school—for just such reasons, it was important to know Wren. We parked, adjusting to the dust like some liberating army, like Maccabbees, in the sudden quiet—quiet and yet, music, faint behind a service door in the garage. I seemed to have already been hearing X, the LA band X, even before the teenaged Konig daughter let us in and confirmed it: Exene's agitated harmony, John Doe's field-holler vibrato—

Sylvie pulled my arm: The family had installed, in Sylvie's honor unless it had belonged to their maid, a brand new art table equipped with a T-square.

"I've been using this chest as a second dresser," the daughter said, bagging clothes in a crouch that also kept time to the music. "But I'm almost done cleaning it out."

Sylvie said, "Oh, I don't even need this many drawers!"

"Really? My God, could I just leave two drawers full? And you can wear anything you want. We can be sisters!" She said it with spirit, but also with a jaded, thespian flourish. "We can get *tipsy*!" She offered a lit joint to the room.

"May I say a quick hi to your folks?" Wren said.

"Wren. Is this one of the seven nights? They're at their thing. Or their other thing."

I joked, "It's four a.m.—do *you* know where your parents are?"

"Services," the daughter said without emotion.

I was trying to decide how she knew to sound exactly this spoiled and yet neglected, because when I was her age I'd only ever failed to be noticed by girls as rich as that. I'd always felt if I could just make a moment's connection, it would be like getting a bike up and rolling, and I could have ridden my life to wherever I wanted it to go.

Also, she was pale, shoulders sunburned from a day at the pool, which made her seem just nerdy enough that being with her might feel platonic, while also not, and so how not to pretend to myself I would soon spend many days with her and Sylvie too? And that Sylvie would still love me and even delight in me for the friendship we would share with the rich neglected Konig girl.

How accepting of life's hurts, how glamorously plain, the band X always managed to sound. Like squatters in some antique LA doll house. After "Soul Kitchen" came "White Girl" and then the immortal "I Must Not Think Bad Thoughts": two chords conversing in endless, fever-dream alternation—if only I'd ever played it for my father. And both chords are finger-picked, like arpeggios, an effect that makes the song at first sound so traipsy it's practically defenseless. But it's the alternating second chord that really gets to you (*I must not think bad thoughts/ What is this world coming to?*), because of

37

the tinged half-step upward it takes, so that you feel the sound might be threatening to lift you away.

Somehow, the girl noticed me loving the song and smiled in agreement, and, for just a second, we seemed to be. . .dancing? For just a second she found nothing unusual about the two of us having this song in common around the Hefty bags of clothes. Beyond the pool, the city shimmered in fragments—Los Angeles, give me some of you!—and I was getting hammered, but then, the Konig girl was, too. When I stumbled a second time, Sylvie caught me, not happily. She had to set down a spaghetti-string top she'd been holding up to herself before a mirror. "It's kind of small," she worried to the girl, and I pulled Sylvie close to say *wear it tonight*, causing her to freak: "This is my new home! They got me that art table. God fucking damn you."

"Wear it anyway," I said, slobbering, and she wrestled me out to the garage.

The Hopeful Twin
Brother Wolf: 2015

EARLY THAT SUMMER I convince a doctor to wean my son off his Zyprexa—it's never helped enough, nothing has—whereupon things head steadily south. Every night brings a Facebook emergency. He posts a song about a father-killer, says my handwriting proves I'm Satan, sends video of a switchblade pressed to the throat of a kitten. Afterward he phones asking if I'll take him to a shooting range. Even he has to chuckle at the timing. What I take to bed is that I got my son to laugh.

Because any laugh you share with your flesh and blood, with the person you welcomed into the world, seems to rejoin, all at once, your whole life history of shared laughter. Something inside of it promises it will outlast every sorrow, because that would just make so much sense. I am gambling we will ride out the transition.

I got the idea from a homeless man I'd talked to outside the St. Luke's meals program. Apparently misdiagnosed, this man had thrown away all antipsychotics, keeping only his mood stabilizer.

Now he was able to wander the world without fear. He kept his whole medical history folded in eighths, like a moldy wallet, in one sock. Philip's doctor is a meek young man named Will Benson who wears checkered shirts straight from their cellophanes. "Your father raises an interesting question, Philip. I tend to agree it's worth a try." Across the room, Philip's mother, Nola, breathes fire.

"*Richard sees him one night a week*," she begins.

Philip crawls his hands up over his ears, and Dr. Will stands up in a nervous way that implies family counseling is down the hall.

That night it's hard to sleep, though, so I go outside and watch the city lights past the cypress trees that line the pool. This is on Mount Washington, where I'm staying with an AA friend. My younger children, from a long second marriage, visit on weekends, rolling out futons in the spare room; Philip fled to his mother's a year ago, complaining about my walls being bugged; and I'm apartment-hunting in LA after two decades of blaming my life on Long Beach. Worrying that my move to Mount Washington shredded the last of my son's mental armor could just be my special talent for taking on guilt. But it also goes without saying that, as the Man with a Plan, I'm culpable for whatever fiasco now comes down.

Whenever my own absent father thought he'd found a short cut in the car—when he took us out sailing, say, even though he couldn't swim—I'd been nothing but proud, taken, enchanted. Shouldn't my son be rooting for me to win? Emilie, the ambivalent girlfriend I've loved for three years—a mystically lithe singer-songwriter who nestles hello, who notices my every vibration—who haunts my dreams—is now just a five-minute drive from where I live.

———

While I'm getting my hair cut near his mom's in Seal Beach, he's outside the salon door gesturing. He's wearing a flimsy black backpack that I maybe prophetically register as a hobo's bindle.

The manicurist asks *May I help you?*, both preemptive and polite, but Philip only wants me.

"I had a fight with Mom," he says outside.

"Oh, Philip. She's probably stressed out. Why don't we go talk to her?"

"Because I can't go back."

"She said this?"

"No."

"Well, okay then. Why can't you?"

We're ten feet from my aging SUV, which I gaze at until I realize he's signaling something. Despite a lifetime of loved ones kicking me under tables, I've always failed to lip read in emergencies. At last he has to whisper in my ear.

They, who can't be named, are coming for him right now, and he needs to escape as far as Oregon, although he has no funds even for a local bus.

I delay answering only so it doesn't look like I never take things in. "And, they've never followed through on any of these threats. Does it help a little to know that?"

He doesn't even look betrayed by my skepticism, which makes me incredibly sad.

"If there's a real chance you're in danger," I continue, "of course I won't leave you at Mom's. But you can't get on a bus to Oregon with no money. Have you even had lunch?"

It's heartbreaking, the priority that food has for my son. Any creature comfort, really. At thirteen, he confessed wanting a wheelchair, just so the family would have to push him. We all howled in outrage, and he laughed alongside us—embarrassed, but not at all converted.

We pick up boxed things at Trader Joe's—kale broccoli salad, a sesame chicken wrap—to eat at a table on the greenbelt like gypsies, as we always have, ever since the divorce when he was two. Over my warnings, he balances a cup of peanut sauce on his knees, and it empties onto his Levi's. Power strollers hike by pushing babies.

"I grant you, Orange County is alienating," I say. "But my gut says six months from now works better. Or a year. That book idea we had, about LA in the eighties? We could get it to an agent."

I trust my own words so deeply that I turn to face him, and my eyes, as Philip once wrote in a school poem, drill holes.

I will always know how to look people in the eye for the sake of my son. One time at Vons, so they'd copy an image of Curious George onto his two-year birthday cake, I got myself to lie, "We own the copyright. H.A. Rey was my grandfather."

"You're not even working on the first chapter," he complains. "You never show me any of it."

"I never show anyone work in progress! Give me a deadline! The point is, with some money, Philip, you could go to Oregon the right way. You'd be an author. You'd have, you know, women."

His silence. It borders on deflation. And the sea breeze is turning cold, so we gather our trash and leave, resurrecting a childhood game of who can fling the Frisbee so it drops into the open trunk of the SUV.

I feel like father of the year by the time Nola opens her front door in an apron. Philip accepts a hug, then skulks to the converted garage where he lives with her Goodwill finds. Lots of wrought iron, lots of antique gowns. Hangers clack and sway whenever he turns in his sleep.

Driving back to Mount Washington, I refocus, calculate the number of car loads that will move me to my next temporary address— this assuming Emilie balks at letting me move in with her in Pasadena. I'm turning sixty on July 4th, and all the people who ever made me feel special on my birthday have died or moved far away, but I manage to feel there's something attractively grownup about this condition.

Indeed, a week later, when I've schlepped my bags to a new house sit, the summer nights are soft, and kids of every race play on the sidewalk, and there's a quiet old man reading the news in the duplex courtyard, and I feel like a happy tourist. But nonstop firecrackers ruin the mood, and once, on a walk around the block, a storefront's plate glass explodes as I pass by.

———————

On the Fourth of July, I've strained my back doing stomach

42

crunches, a problem Emilie turns sexy, dropping off a gluten-free carrot cake and making out with me on the floor where I lie. I can't do much to excite her in return, which I worry is a little too fine with her.

Afterward she floats around slicing us cake and refilling our coffee—before returning to her kids and their holiday plans, leaving me to mine.

As for my other kids—Daniel is thirteen at this time, Zooey eleven—we follow the traffic to the Army base in Los Alamitos, where we're the only family without blanket or chairs: a distinction that formerly made me feel young and hip. I feel stirred by the Marine Corps singers. A good dose of Motrin is allowing me to be playful—hurling tennis balls to my children over the throngs.

It's in the chill of dusk, the suspended violet fugue before the first rockets wriggle upward, that I find both my hidden sadness and who it's about. I'm in pain that I haven't brought Philip. I'm guilty despite the fact his paranoia in crowds would have made it all but impossible. He'd even agreed with me on that point. But the fact remained I was the one who raised it.

Now I'm no longer marveling at the fireworks, only adding to the thousands of them I've seen in my life, till it's time to leave.

And the voicemails that crash in when I charge my phone at home are all from Nola. At first she sounds halting, withholds details. Then she's panicky. Then pleading. The PET team has been called. He's painting swastikas on the windows. This will be the phone number of the nurse's station.

I am moved by Nola's bravery; I want to thank her for handling yet another tragic emergency with our son, before I realize that what she's doing is the opposite of reaching out.

She will visit only the first two days of his hospitalization. (Here are his things. This is the list of his other prescriptions. I can't do it anymore. Time for you to man up.) If I ask whether she's all right, she gathers her forces to pretend that no one spoke.

Philip's curls have been cut so short they could bleed—Nola's last backfired kindness. In the lockup courtyard, he rests his forehead on a school-cafeteria table, jerks upright at loudspeaker announcements.

He gesticulates about the nurse who is promising to kill him.

The high point of Philip's hospitalization will be texting Emilie from the wheel of my car. *I GOT THEM TO PRESCRIBE CLOZARIL!*

Remind me? Is that the good one?

The gold standard! Tightly regulated because of a rare lethal side effect. Infinitesimally rare.

With luck it may be mere days before this wonder drug will uncase my happy son.

High point 2 is getting him out. I arrange for a bed at an independent living home in North Long Beach called, stucco-gothically, The Gables. He "passes" a semiconscious hospital-bed interview with the apartment's manager, a woman who despite multiple tattoos has the haircut of a helping professional.

"Dude," I say, as we depart the double doors, "you're falling upward. You're getting an apartment."

It's a ghetto lanai sort of building, the kind where a certain idea of California paradise has been memorialized. But there are signs in the neighborhood that I try to find hopeful. A Mexican cantina. A vacant lot with pasture fencing.

Naturally the manager, Robin, isn't around when we pull up, but I can't let Philip detect my worry. "Hello!" I call cheerfully through the locked front gate.

A one-legged black kid crutches over to let us in. Behind him, an older man, whiskery-wolfish like Red Foxx, asks if I have a minute, and then stands cogitating, as if unsure what to do with the opportunity. On the excuse of my son, I slip by.

———————

It takes a few trips to get the bags of clothes upstairs. "You want these in drawers or hung?" I ask.

What he wants, he says, is some darkness, except that the curtain, a blue beach towel, doesn't span the window. I peek through the gap at the rehabby scene outside. There's a row of vending machines, a torn vinyl couch. Residents aren't allowed to smoke pot, but a sense of retro hippie promise seems to waft throughout—and then, in chilling moments, departs, like an airlift of GIs. At the room's tiny desk, Philip sits studiously eating shelled pistachios, while I teach myself to sort his medication on the extra bed. The pills migrate like ball bearings across the lumpy mattress.

For a bedside table, I set up a folding chair. There I position a book at an angle that would invite someone to read it.

Then I need to get him his room key. Robin answers her unit door this time. But instead of providing a key of Philip's own, she fronts me hers, making me swear we won't lose it—half insult, half favor. I return to Philip's room, feeling all the sorrow of a father who has no key to give his son.

"I'm gonna go," I say. "But I'll be back in the morning. I love you, Philip."

He only nods goodbye.

The whiskery neighbor hails me when I'm outside. "Boss, let me, let me ask you—" I smile like a deaf foreigner, but he hurries to catch up. "Which way you heading, man?"

"Sorry, hurrying. Anyway, my car's overstuffed. With clothes and kitchen things."

"You don't got ten minutes?" It's a cringing smile—what kind of creature doesn't have ten minutes? Finally he eases off. "That was your son, huh? He's a smart kid, looks like."

I give a knowing, caregiver shrug. "He wants to go back to school, if he can get well enough. He's a writer. I'm a writer—I teach writing. You guys all need to take care of each other." I look him in the eye as gravely as I can. "I hope you guys all take care of each other."

"Well, now that we've met, I definitely will. I'm *gonna* look after your boy."

"Richard," I say, and we shake hands.

"Lewis."

As I fumble for the gate's deadbolt, the young guy with one leg crutches over again to help. "That's my boy," Lewis says. "He's a good one too." But I'm not clear if he means boy as in son.

45

I look up at Philip's window. "Hang on," I say, and I march back upstairs. Late sunlight inflames the blue towel window covering.

"I don't remember if I told you, Philip, but the pill organizer will be right here." I lay it on the folding chair beside his bed. I swivel the chair.

"And your phone is charging next to it." I whisper: "Your wallet's in the drawer of the captain's bed. You hear me? This drawer. Unless the drawer's not good. I just wouldn't leave the wallet out."

"I'll probably go to bed in a few minutes," he says.

"All right, then," I say, but I don't leave. "Text me when you've taken your med?" He has to get this dose in him.

He nods, bleary. I mustn't make him feel he's being pushed.

At the doorway I pause to text the manager:

FYI – Philip left your key on his windowsill. I'll be by tomorrow to pay rent.

Ok no problem

Wondering – in exchange for extra rent, would you be able to give him a friendly reminder to take his meds.

It takes a long time, but she answers: *Sure.* (No attempt to waive the money, either.)

Thank you, so much.

An hour later, from my house-sit, I'll text again: *FYI – His bedtime meds are in organizer on nightstand.*

Normally I don't do this I will however check on him

I remind her: *I can pay you.*

But there's nothing more for a good three minutes. Finally the screen lights:

Done

With a happy emoji.

I fire back my own row of emojis—clapping hands and two thumbs up—to which Robin replies *UR welcome* with a halo, and then: *Movie time with my daughter.*

This relic of normalcy does its work; we're old-time parents, bonding over family rituals, overcoming our snipey beginning.

———————

The next day I visit, and the next, but we keep winding up at the empty Mexican cantina in the middle of the afternoon. Thereafter we begin stationing at my house-sit, where I read the apartment listings on Craigslist, one eye on the calendar. Four weeks before I return to teach. The kitchen mantle is a standing desk for the sake of my back.

In passing, I steal glances at my work. It's a book of magazine adventures, showing their age, that sold somehow to a tiny local press. A copyeditor from a freelance collective has kneecapped a closing line from heaven. The chairman of Conde Nast swooned for that line! But I'm only love-hate mad. It's the crafting-and-polish, the back and forth—Bailey Kavanagh's definition of bliss. Two lucky minds unshrouding a printer's plate that was composed before time. You want to share a cigarette after.

It's almost embarrassing that this is what I was helplessly born to do, both badly and well, regardless what detours I've taken through the years. Regardless of the summer acting class before marrying Nola, or my one improbable airline commercial. Regardless of one audition as a bearded cigarette smoker, when bearded men smoked cigarettes on billboard ads. (My visage was deemed "biblical," not alpha-dude, not the object of bromance.)

Regardless of my stint as a public radio correspondent, antagonizing the newsroom and listeners with some on-air folksy bafflement about the fashions of PC.

There was even a side hustle designing mosaic tables. I wasn't neurotic enough about these things—maybe that was why they bored me.

Philip asks if he can stay overnight.

"When I get my own place," I say carefully, "and you're stabilizing on the meds. Then we'll definitely have that talk."

"Listen a minute," Lewis says one day outside the Gables, with the one-legged boy beside him. "You said you teach writing? If you want some good ideas—some ideas that would make you rich, you get what I mean? You should read what that boy does. Science-fiction stuff."

"Hey, wow," I say, because there could be an ally in all this for Philip.

"Yeah, he writes good—he just doesn't know how to put things down in the right—the way you're supposed to. But if someone, you get what I'm saying, someone like you helps him with that part, I'm telling you. You'd both get rich."

"Well, honestly," I say—it's what I've learned to tell people —"the best thing is for him to register in the fall for classes. If he can get himself there."

On the apartment front, I start to wonder if the people who offer me advice might be rubbing something in. Nola, who is otherwise unresponsive, forwards links to singles buildings in places like Hawaiian Gardens or Paramount. A shrink whom Philip used to see says we should live walking distance to Philip's blood draw in the city of Downey. A friend in Long Beach lets me sleep on his couch, but only Wednesdays. "You just need six other friends each week— doncha have six other friends?" In the same buckaroo tone, he now asks, "Whyncha stay in a motel till you find what you want?"

But a motel would eat my last month's rent deposit in a week, and I'm angry he doesn't know it.

Another old buddy cares too much and is years behind the curve. "There's a thing called board and care," he recites from his notes, and I tell him I haven't got time. Stanley was a roots rock and roller, and he still has the hair and the western shirts but is elderly in the voice in a way that underscores when he's righteous. "This is what I know. You need to not lash out at people who are trying to help you."

Philip stirs in the king-sized bed.

"I'll get you back to the Gables in a little while," I say.

In the silence, our thoughts sometimes drift like fingers toward each other's hand. "You have to stop staring at people, Philip," I say as I drive. "You're staring at me again."

"I'm sorry," he says, and then, suddenly, "I guess it's because I'm lonely. I start to have thoughts about things that I don't want to value, because it's better not to."

I take the odd sentence in slowly. "You mean—thoughts like, feeling that we're close?

"Yes," he says.

"Because you think it's easier to be cynical?"

"No. But I aspire to be. Cynical." He says it like he means business.

I find that I'm starting to cry, which he probably finds embarrassing.

"Do you know what I mean?" he asks—he's so vulnerable again, trusting, it's like my son is back. Then he coughs—he's been coughing a lot, I notice.

"Yeah, I do know. I love you, Philip," and my voice breaks. "I'm worried we were foolish not to get a blood test for your cough."

"What difference does it make if I die? I'm not saying I'm suicidal. My life is not going to go anywhere."

"Well," I say, "I don't agree. There's a chance that the best is in front of you. I think you could have a good life. You could be a good author." My voice gives way. "I'm sorry. I'm crying because I don't like seeing you in pain, and..."

He shakes his head. "I know that you're crying for your own reasons."

Uh-oh. "What do you mean?"

"It's okay."

"Philip, I'm crying because I don't like to see you in pain! And I guess because when they say your meds can have a rare side effect, it makes me think of what it would be like to lose you."

"I thought you already knew I was going to die. I thought that was the point."

"The point?"

"Of Clozaril. That's why it's named that."

"I'm not getting this."

"Like in baseball," he says knowingly, and then he reverts to a harried whisper. "The pitcher."

Closer. Clozaril.

"No, no, oh, Philip. I can't imagine that's the idea. I'm sure it wasn't named for that. No, no, no!"

Above us twirls a sign: The Panda Garden, at Atlantic and Carson. At least it isn't the cantina. We pull in to eat and I talk him down further. I'm hoping to turn this narrow escape into one of our jokes on the Leviton men. I'm furious with God that this could have gone either way. The tenuousness of human rescue.

"Trust me, if you were in the focus group when they were naming this medicine, they definitely wouldn't have named it Clozaril!"

Philip settles in, distracted, to his rice.

———————

Realizing that even a misread fortune cookie could trigger him, I elect to pay quickly at the counter. It's still light outside as I lead Philip, like some very dejected VIP, across another restaurant parking lot to our SUV.

The next morning when I pick him up, he's already had breakfast, and a bad experience. "Two cars tried to run me down in the crosswalk," he seethes, slamming and locking the door from inside. When Philip gets into cars, he's a fireball of energy, then pays for the expenditure by feeling depleted.

I interrogate. How do we know these cars were actually aiming?

"Because I saw the drivers' eyes."

"I'm going back and counting your pills," I announce, not even caring if he feels accused by my U-turn.

But upstairs, Philip's pill tray shows he's missed only one dose all week.

That's when I realize: The increments. Philip's Clozaril dose was supposed to be walked upward, daily, from the first dose he received in the hospital. But on the day of his release, the outpatient pharmacy dispensed as if Day 1. We're moving backwards. He's at risk for a full psychotic break.

"Listen to me, Philip," I say, gathering up his bag of pills. "Fuck. Fuck."

After burning rubber back to the housesit, I phone Dr. Will, pulling him out of a meeting—I'm not just another caregiver to trample.

"You see that something has to be done. We agree on that, right?"

"The thing is, though, there's no system, no protocol for –"

"For fixing a mistake?" I give a tortured laugh. "Doctor, is that even—Hippocratic?"

He admits, "No." But thinking aloud through the iffy logistics does not get him the traction he'd like. "I'd have to obtain the titrated difference," he says, "of a tightly regulated, *tightly regulated* substance that can only be released by the pharmacy in Downey, and we're all due to meet at his mandatory discharge meeting at two in Lomita, which is hours from Downey in traffic, but," and he gives a series of concessionary sighs that suggest he's only complaining about his day.

I gaze out the window of my house-sit, from which any freeway is a maddening summer obstacle course away, a course of road crews and walker patients, and transients pedaling slowly on bicycles with American flags on the backs. "What if the patient was in your hospital, doctor, and needed this drug? Are you saying it couldn't be done?"

"I'll see what we can do," he says. "Can I reach you at this number?" In a few more minutes his nurse, Eric, calls me, and all the men are on board.

"Bring his old meds," Eric says. "The doctor will replace them with the corrected dose."

"I heard. I hear him in the background."

"Bring the meds." And we hang up.

Thanking them both in my heart, I dig through our black bag of prescriptions. Incredibly, I can't find the old pills.

The bag is turned out, the bag is turned in.

I shake Philip on the king size bed. "Up. Now. Sorry. I may have left your PILLS at the GABLES, and now we're—. Son of a—"

Nor are the pills among the belongings in the back of my SUV, the socks and liquefied coconut oil and the loose tennis balls and kitchen spices.

Midmorning still, but nearing noon, late enough for us to be hungry already—how does anyone do anything but deal with getting food?

At last we reach the Gables, but something's off. For one thing, the gate stands unlocked—the courtyard gives off a dusty, high-noon impression. From someplace hidden, we hear a wet, roaring rant, reverberating like a sprain, neither far off nor close. It's as though a ventriloquist, ironing out some weird bug in his act, has instead made himself disappear.

"Hello!" I call, whanging on the screen to Philip's shared, three-bedroom unit. Both of Philip's housemates can be glimpsed through a gap in the drapes. With each bang, they freeze, until the one named Arnold loosens the chain. "We thought you were Lewis."

"What's wrong with Lewis?"

"Aw, he's drunk!" Arnold says, sounding like the owner of a dead jalopy. "When he drinks, he accuses everyone of owing him money."

Arnold suffers a panicky form of OCD, which he channels into marathon bursts of janitorial work, splashing buckets of Lysol onto counters and floors.

The upstairs housemate, Greg, trudges in slow, steady circles, as if he's being marched for another man's crime. "Two more weeks in California and I'm done with these goddamn criminals."

At this moment, Lewis's voice nears the window. *Motherfucker, mess you up!*

The ruckus then passes to a next unit and a next.

It's hard to convey how perfectly suspended between misery and peace these middle-aged sufferers appear. How cheated by life, and how accustomed to it.

"I wanted to see Santa Monica before I leave," George says. "Have you been to Santa Monica?" He's holding a map book that he picked up from a Holiday Inn.

"That would require a lot of buses," I say, edging past him to Philip's room, where I check for the lost pills. They're not on the windowsill, not on the desk with the drifts of pistachio shells. Not in the captain's bed drawer or on the folding-chair nightstand. Not in jean pockets or jacket pockets—it's hopeless, I decide, cursing, and now we hear sirens.

Inasmuch as Lewis probably wants to keep me for a future touch; inasmuch as the last thing we need is to get trapped here during a police action, I decide it's safe to get Philip outside, slip out through the gate to my car. It's been another futile trip.

"Where are we going now?" Philip asks when we're almost to the ocean.

"South on Atlantic," I say, just to be a jerk to someone. (This afternoon, I tell myself. The curve of his life will point upward.)

"You know what?" I say. "We've got about an hour before we head toward Kaiser. There are rental listings in my shirt pocket. I might look at a couple in Belmont Shore."

But do I want Philip to come in with me, if we do? He seems to be wearing the jeans with the spilled sauce from the park. My phone chimes twice and I pull over.

Asked the owners about your request to pay by the week they said they might but its gonna cost extra. $15 a week more So its due do you know if he's staying another month

I'll know more in a couple days, I reply to Robin. Then I feel my anger rise. *Is Lewis still going to be there?*

He's evicted. Gone as of today. Leave the check in the garage office with my wife.

Wife? The woman in the garage office wears a spiked collar and misspells receipts on a Speed Racer note pad. These facts make the neighborhood feel ten degrees hotter and ten miles farther from Mount Washington.

I will, I text back, engine idling. There's a backup of cars waiting to turn right onto Ocean, nobody moving. I nudge my way into one lane and the next, slipping into the queue, but traffic remains a crawl.

"This isn't going to work," I say. "We'd better get to Kaiser."

But crews have blocked traffic toward the Vincent Thomas Bridge—there's a fire in Edison's underground electrical vaults, says the traffic cop. Servers are down, Siri unavailable, so I can't even navigate a short cut. There's only a very long way around, if I take the 710 to the 405 to the 110 to PCH, through Wilmington.

I consider telling the cop about our situation, the way my father might have, medical black bag on the seat beside him, and watch that phantom of privilege vaporize in the heat. By the time we get onto the 710 we're running dangerously late, and for the second time this week, I'm beginning to cry—simultaneously trying to remember, because I'm sure people have been here before me, how to make falling apart a good thing. I explain certain facts to God: that I'm sixty years old, doing all the footwork I know how to do. As proof, I submit these tears.

"Let's try not to get anybody killed," I say to Philip. What dramas might I be triggering with these words?

———————

Dr. Will's air-conditioned office, where we arrive eighteen minutes late, is as close as the twenty-first century HMO affords to a scene of backroom dealing. Eric the nurse welcomes us in, then pivots to corral the doctor, hand already extended for the drop off of old pills, which I have to credibly explain I've lost.

The news lands personally, and not happily, on Eric's shoulders. His estimation of my character has possibly been the fulcrum on which our whole agreement rests. "You . . . can't *find them?*" he repeats.

As if in time lapse, I watch Dr. Will age a little further into his ethical land of no return.

Still, it takes not a minute's thought in any direction to conclude that our least complicated option is to stumble forward, football players after a broken play.

Then Philip and I emerge into the afternoon haze of Lomita. There's a Jack in the Box in the same parking lot, where I sit him down with a large soda to wash down the lifegiving medication. While he sips, I step outside to phone a few more apartments, spying through the restaurant window on my son, alone, motionless. How does anybody sit that riveted by a cup and a straw?

Can anybody know the absurd pride I feel? The tragedy, the special beauty of him just as he is? Is it merely the tragedy of us all, only unique because he's mine? I almost snap a photo to post on Facebook.

But I know he would feel ripped off.

By the time we hit the Gables, around seven, street parking is scarce enough that we have to park a block away and walk, and against the low setting sun we see the silhouette of a shuffling, swaggering man.

"Hey, now," Lewis hails us.

"Lewis, I heard what happened." Ambiguous solidarity seems the only way to go. "Where will you be staying?"

"Where am I *staying?* Where *would* I stay? I'm staying right here!"

"Oh. Robin had said—have I misunderstood?"

"Listen to me," he says. "These fuckers gonna talk tough every time. *Every* time. You think I don't I know my rights?" He winks. "*You and I* know that. I *know* you know—right?"

But the next day, when I look to Robin for answers, she only shrugs—a fellow victim now. "*I* don't even want to be here anymore," she says, with shit-kicker frankness. "As soon as I can get out—"

"Oh, no," I say. *Don't leave us,* is all I can think.

"Just sayin' you're right to be upset."

Something in her compassion sounds less than straightforward, though. She's in the doorway of her unit, one foot tapping and her teeth a little on edge. Suddenly she motions me inside. We're just an inch inside her place. "The cashbox just got stolen," she whispers. "And my car. Anyway, the owners probably think I faked it." She turns away, one eye looking back for my reaction.

"Are police looking for your car?"

She sucks on a cigarette. "Oh, Christ, no. I already found it, a block away! They got some clothes and CDs is all." She makes a slightly sympathetic face, to convey that my naiveté is sadder than her loss. "It's just, your kid is nice. I'm on your side. I can see why you'd want him out of here."

I put aside the incongruous sensation that, in an earlier decade, we'd be about to kiss. I erase the tattoos and her halter top and try to locate the corresponding scene from the seventies teen movie that the housing project pays its homage to.

"I'm looking for places," I say. "I'm working on it."

55

"Yeah? In Seal Beach?" She's forever stuck on that detail of Philip's past. It excites her to assume that he skateboards.

"We're looking all over the place, basically."

"Here," she says, fishing a card from her purse. "I haven't told anybody else. This board and care near City College has a bed. He can go to school. He can *skateboard* to school."

"Do me a favor," I say to Philip in the car. "Open my Maps."

"Siri!" he shouts at my phone. "Siri!—"

His timing is off, so the app won't open.

"You do it," he groans, but instead I pull over and use my thumbs.

I don't love what I see. The address is not near the college's main campus, but its seedy satellite. In the name of faith, I suppose, I don't turn around.

It's the inevitable board-and-care courtyard. The raving masses wearing trunks and jerseys from mismatched sports. A deafening loudspeaker, like from a submarine movie, orders a janitor from accident A to accident B.

In honor of the demoralized director, Tatiana, I pretend to be thoughtful, pretend to measure drapes. A day room features a large box TV, blaring ads for injury law firms.

"Robin," I say when we're back, so calmly I surprise myself. "You've actually been to Chez Bon?"

"Oh, yeah." she says, poker faced.

"Then, of course, therefore, you know that it's a death sentence."

She appears to be a little thrown by my honesty—and then, because I don't react to her expression, she looks entirely not thrown. She'll offer any face I want.

"I wanted you to see the contrast," she says, opting for shrewd. "I wanted you to see you can't be choosy."

I could throw a punch, right here, only I'm not certain I even believe that Robin means this. And my son is looking flushed and stranded, and exposed, like a pale prisoner forced to change clothes behind a towel.

We climb upstairs, Philip's arms dangling limp at his sides. At least they're not rigid, I think, not like when we tried him on Abilify. The temperature jumps ten degrees by the upper landing.

"Is Mom coming to visit soon?" he asks, pulling bedcovers to his neck despite the heat.

Nola has an older son, cerebral and sweet, with an Asperger-like syndrome, and I'm astonished I haven't thought to text him till this moment.

Ronan, I type, *is anyone there well enough to let me know if Nola is OK? She left very upset and shaky last week, and I haven't heard from her since.*

I will call her, he replies.

So I wait, while Philip shuts his eyes. It's a few minutes before I get Ronan's earnest follow-up.

I was able to reach her, but I unfortunately cannot remember what she said to tell you.

I burst into a laugh. I can't help it. "Philip, you'd love this!" It's as if we still chuckle at such things all the time.

But he's gone to sleep. I kiss his forehead once and leave.

Are there good things about my being a vagabond? The soreness of sleeping on floors, on air mattresses, is becoming, itself, sleep-enhancing. My next two nights, exhausting every resource, are on the art studio floor at my old editor Bailey Kavanagh's in LA. Even my breathing seems to upset the sanctuary of her singlehood.

Then comes a week at the Long Beach home of a lady who takes off to be with her boyfriend if I'll care for her two dogs. Despite knowing that I'm ten days from starting fall semester as a homeless professor, she texts daily to ask if I'm enjoying the relaxation.

I'm expecting another such text when I hear from Philip instead. It isn't good.

Dad, they're showing my room?

This is, Robin confirms, no delusion.

Eli my boss will help with placement we are closing the Gables down.

Why? And when?

Converting to Section 8 we are closing by the first I can try and team

57

him with a group that's staying if u like? I'll have my boss call you. Or you can try him but not after five they're Orthodox Jews.

Born a Jew, I'm thinking one thought only: I must catch the eye of these owners. I must hail their entourage, touch the hem of somebody's garment. But when I arrive at The Gables, a silver Mercedes is already pulling away, undoubtedly theirs. It could not possibly help my cause to give screaming chase.

The gate stands wide open this time, tenants everywhere.

"Stomp your feet when you walk past Unit 4," Robin welcomes me, walking in staccato. "They have bed bugs."

"Wait. Isn't that where Philip's being moved?"

"Ugh," Robin says, though it's not clear if it's in understanding or impatience. "Don't stress. I haven't even been home all morning."

A blond man who reminds me of a camp director stands in the center of a circle of bewildered tenants, handing out cards for a downtown sober living. The scene is that of a third world airport. Philip's guitar has already been moved to the new unit, and a conversation is in progress with the one-legged boy about local punk bands.

"You need to meet this man," I say to my son, but the camp director calls out, "How you doin', Killer?" in a voice so big that Philip scurries behind a bush. This escape assigns no more blame than a pigeon does creating distance from a child.

"We're going to see the place anyway," I tell Philip. "We can't afford not to."

"I can't share a room," he says.

It's true. In his imagination or otherwise, every shared room is an extension of a bullying ritual begun in middle school.

I look for Robin, who's suddenly vanished. My thumbs crush the touchscreen.

These are mentally fragile renters who need stability! You told him he'd fit here! You knew about him, you interviewed him. He is frightened.

I'm sorry I feel bad he is a good kid. Make him talk to Carl. He would be around people his age skateboarding etc

"We're just going to look. Okay?" I say to Philip.

Downtown Long Beach, through a certain filter, can emit a funky, backstreet grace. It's like the cities of my twenties as I romantically saw them: San Francisco, Sacramento. It's a past I've dangled before Philip many times. Not far is a Food Not Bombs collective with a tire swing in the backyard. A girl broke Philip's heart there when he was a senior in high school.

Inside Carl's sober living, the guys on the leather couch are of a certain wayfarer mold, reciting 12-Step wisdoms when asked about their plans. On the TV is an action thing with Charles Bronson. Philip roams the interior not too fearfully, though he doesn't interact. Airy Victorian bedrooms have been reconverted with Home Depot fixtures. A locked walk-in pantry is where Carl keeps all the meds. "How many times a day do you take medication, Philip?" Carl asks.

"I prefer not to live here," Philip recites, Bartleby-like.

"Hey, no worries." We watch Carl banish all drama from his brow, pretending to watch birds cavort in trees. "Why don't you take your time and think about it?"

"What don't you get," I say as we return to The Gables, chopping my words like a machete, *"about needing to keep our options open."*

"He told me he wanted to kill me," Philip says. "He blinked his eyes in code."

The one-legged boy, crutching across the courtyard to admit us, asks, "Is it amazing? I heard some of the guys say it's amazing."

I ask if he's going to go see the place too.

He surveys the empty courtyard uncertainly, then reassures us, "I think someone's supposed to take me."

———

That night Emilie comes to Long Beach for her daughter's soccer tournament, a rare convergence (she's the ride to, her ex is the ride back), and she wonders if, despite (or because of) all that's going on, I'd want to be together. Maybe grab a bite after the awards. She can't hang out super late, even though it's the ex's custodial weekend, because if their daughter goes to sleep early and their 15-year-old son needs a ride back from Fiona Apple at Largo, Emilie might prefer to pick up the son rather than make her ex throw their daughter in his car. Her every verb—hang, grab, wonder, prefer—is from a foreign America.

Into the phone, at a not quite detectable volume, I want to say: Your life is overwhelming. How may I pitch in? Instead I say it would be a miracle to see her face, however briefly. Which is, humiliatingly, true.

Nearly every day she's served as sounding board on the phone— sometimes for hours, sequestered from her kids—but only from a distance. She is stepping into Pilates. She is stepping outside a party to say, *"Just a bookmark for now but I wish I could hug you."*

The soccer tournament takes place at the park where Philip lost his virginity. His high school girlfriend, now a dancer at City College, lay down with him behind some bushes and got pregnant. Philip was slender then, before all the metabolic changes, wearing a ribbed thermal undershirt, but breast tissue from Risperidone was raising a mound of fabric across the front. The swelling could look buff, until he turned to the side. He was a handsome, nervous boy, watching out for all the rival lovers he'd been hearing on the phone wires.

I always spot Emilie before she spots me. In sunglasses, she wanders a grass field like a celebrity who's lost her handler. Her hoodie is lint-free, her lips glossy and fresh. But when you reach her, she's funny and joshing you for not hugging like you know who she is.

"You're sweaty," she says with concern.

"Oh, shit. I'm sorry."

"No, no! I'm not complaining. Jesus! Now you're mad!"

"I'm not mad," I say, but she can't tell, because I haven't smiled. "No, I'm just—I'm sure I'm very sweaty. Anyway."

"What should we do?" she says, after we've stood a few seconds. "Eat first and walk? Walk to eat?"

"I wouldn't mind a walk," I say, looking around. "Of course, if you don't want to walk, that's fine, too."

We stroll halfway around the park in the twilight; we cross Carson Street to get tacos for dinner, and then, feeling sadly jaunty, I offer a driving tour of apartments I've applied for. We drive from

Lakewood down to Spring, past the airport to the 405, to the 710 downtown, then toward the university. I point out the leafy crow's nest in the arts village with stairs as steep and narrow as a fire ladder. A couple in their twenties had sat on a futon couch so blankly that I eventually derived they were high. Or maybe only putting their conversation on hold until I left. Maybe they were breaking up. Maybe that was why they were moving out.

I point through the windshield at the apartment where five tenants have to jockey their cars backward into traffic from a barber shop's driveway to let each other out. I am dreaming this all could sound impressive to the woman I was angling to live with a few weeks before.

Emilie can't glean much through a car window, of course. But she's happy for me if I'm excited to be going for something high-density and urban. Is this what I want? she asks.

I don't know what I want, only what I wanted. The distance between "happy for" and "happy with" feels transcontinental.

We kiss goodnight at her car, and then I lead her to the freeway toward Pasadena, watching her in the rear-view mirror, releasing the visual tow rope, until she's on the onramp and out of view.

I can't bear, now, going back to care for someone's dogs. In a minimart parking lot, as if finding candy in my jacket pocket, it occurs to me to text some fighting words to Robin.

By law that unit must be sanitary. I am a 40-year veteran journalist. Look me up online. I will rain holy hell.

Obviously the threat is empty. Isn't it? My stomach ties up, just for old time's sake, as if a deadline has just been assigned. I could dial, you know, my Mount Washington friend, the one who knows the one who won the Pulitzer for writing about the homeless oboist who got named unhoused-activist-in-residence at UCLA. I know just where he is on a Friday night, I can see his phone on the table of a hip Highland Park taco place. I think of a time I tagged along, the footloose boarder beside three couples. One of them, hearing how footloose I was, asked if I was handy, because they'd just renovated a building in East L.A. to get in on the gentrification, and they needed a manager. For more rent than I could ever dream of paying, plus repairs, I could herald that a Starbucks (or hot yoga?) is on its way.

But when I arrive the next morning to check on Philip in the dreaded Unit 4, it isn't the mess that I notice.

"Didn't you live across the courtyard?" I ask Lewis.

He looks up from a boxspring to see me. "I know how to talk to them."

He's not asleep, nor even drunk, but flipping face down as if for comfort, he has sprawled himself absurdly in both directions, limbs stretched territorially to the walls.

Toward the kitchen, the one legged-boy lies facedown, half on a pile of sheets, half off, his crutches strewn where they fell. His weariness seems epic, his rest a preview of heaven. Robin stands over, attempting to roust him. "We have to spray. I am so sorry to do this."

"Actually," I say to Lewis, "Philip's supposed to be up here."

"Oh yeah? I think they got an extra bed they could set up. Maybe you could ask?" He adds, "You know I like your son. He'll be fine here. Where you staying? You moving in here too?"

Philip moans—for a man of six foot three, he accommodates himself so obediently to life's checkerboard—then trudges up the stairs of his old unit, now draped in painter throws. The big man from Oregon waits outside his own bedroom, in standby mode, as if there's been an accident or a flood.

"Seriously," he says as we pass. "Your son is the best housemate I've ever had."

———————

When I've been turned down for nine straight apartments, I start to question if my prayers are even heard. There are such things, the Bible says, as curses, demons, mighty spiritual warriors with flaming arrows. Once, when I'd rented office space in a crumbling mainline church, the evangelical friend who picked me up there for lunch got knocked backward at my office door. He sniffed the air like a bloodhound and then asked if I'd let him pray over my computer. "Sometimes these old churches. . . How can you *work* in here?" he'd said.

I miss who I was the day that I let this man pray. I long for the way of eternally childlike belief. I'd been a member, with him, of the men's marriage accountability group at his church.

My second wife's church. I spent ten years there. Nola surely enjoyed holding her tongue about that.

So I phone there. "That's intense," young Pastor Brent says of my situation. This is what I mean about young.

He puts me in touch with the Sozo prayer team of Lorrie and Gabi, who tell me they don't normally do such triage on a Friday, but who also seem, unmistakably, to relish the emergency.

And suddenly it's like I never left. The windowless carpeted room. The semicircle of chairs both folding and beanbag. The locked cabinets of Goldfish crackers. Lorrie, a former policewoman, will be the lead investigator, Gabi the note-taking technician, watching for movements of the divine.

Sozo prayer, as Lorrie explains it, is impressively systematic: an inventory of blockages on the order of chakras. *Whom haven't I forgiven? Where have I not forgiven me? Who do I say God is?*

As we explore my childhood, my marriages, my bosses, my professional disappointments, I roll out my skillful absolutions. Then, suddenly, we hit a root nerve, and I'm sobbing authentically. It unfolds that the thing I most desperately envied growing up, the thing I envied the way Lex Luthor envies Superboy, is what I've failed to give my children: A stable marriage in a stable home.

It's one for the Sozo annals, of course, that the demon I've just named is also my presenting complaint—homelessness. This sets off a lot of knowing eye contact between Lorrie and Gabi. And though I don't know how any of this changes the nine turndowns, I know it's unlikely that a better stopping point is in the cards. I only want to stay in the honesty of my guilt, like it's a home in itself. Although always with prayer there remains this hope of postponement, this not wanting yet to reenter the mess of your life.

In the parking lot, they hand me a printed sheet of Biblical affirmations, phrased as proof of how God is said to love me, and what's surprising, here, isn't the stillness that follows me to my car. What's surprising is that for a moment, my stillness doesn't actually care if I ever solve my housing problem.

Recognizing this to be a higher grade of stillness, I decide I'd better savor it. I drive not yet in the direction of my house-sit, instead traveling south along Redondo to Second Street, where I stop and park. It's a Friday night in Belmont Shore. The usual beachy vagabonds loiter by the bars. Tweens eat cinnamon buns in paper trays. To their overfed families, I feel a sudden allegiance. But it isn't that I want to be like them. I just want them to feel as purged for one moment of their lives as I feel for this moment of mine.

I remember the throwaway newspaper they used to have, back when I'd call the neighborhood "Bedford Falls"—I meant the wholesome Bedford Falls, from *It's A Wonderful Life*, not the one that's turned rotten because Jimmy Stewart wasn't there to help them. I get out of the car and cross at a light and try to decide if it's normal to see what I've always seen: two towns at once who look like phantoms to each other, the safe people in one and the vagabond people at the gate.

Behold, it still exists, this freebie newspaper—*The Grunion Gazette*—stacked right there inside its coinless rack. Leaning against the machine in the summer air, I unfold the pages, the dwindling classifieds.

"You're a professor?" says a landlord I phone the next morning. He's astounded at his own good luck.

———

It must be my birthday, because it's clearly the Fourth of July, but for some reason that I can't explain, it's Philip's birthday too. The firing range at the Alamitos Army base is closed for the holiday, but Eli, the caretaker, has agreed to hide his keys beneath a rock where we can find them. We wander inside, unbox our weapons from hot crates and aim them, lawless and unhindered. The heat is surreal, astonishing, and we've shed every kind of armor, clothes, skins, even our very weight. We see a large, fallen horse with one lame leg, a horse beset by agonies, and we fire a mercy shot each into its neck, father and son, but in the flash of the explosion the animal is made whole.

———————

Not until I wake up Philip to leave The Gables—he's supine on his captain's bed, on clouds of bunched-up comforter—do I realize that Lewis, quite logically, may have taken possession of Unit 4 merely in order to stay close to his son. Assuming, of course, that the one-legged boy is Lewis's literal son.

In any case, I see neither of them here today, which spares us all an awkward goodbye.

Outside, the line of Section 8 applicants has formed at the gate. They move aside, with what strikes me as tense courtesy, for Philip and me to pass.

That Saturday, Emilie visits our new apartment in its unfurnished, squatter phase. The dimensions, the balcony are palatial. "It's nice!" she says, pacing the living room, which is empty but for two temporary futons. "Do you feel good about it? I mean, still?"

I say I do, with a sigh of qualification that is meant to remind her about the calamity that has chosen my son.

When Philip takes his evening meds and passes out—his cough beginning to trouble me greatly—I walk with Emilie to dinner at a sidewalk bistro that adjoins the independent record store. She wears a white textured peasant top, her arms and shoulders as flawless as a child's. Over salmon and asparagus, I tell her my experience from the church classroom, and suspiciously, for one of the only times in our relationship, I don't need to translate the jargon of desperate belief. "You look so good right now," she keeps saying, something I often have been told when I am about to go away.

What is brown with the palest possible pink? Those are the two colors combined in Emilie. It's a lovely, suspended interlude and I seem to notice everything—end of summer, date night, sidewalks thronged. In the setting sun, the transients appear more like touristy carousers. Emilie takes my hand, tuning out the hordes, and we're a couple of miraculous beings when we touch and release, fingers thick and musical, before I begin my new future with my son. It's a toast to the end of romance.

Sometimes, reflecting on Lewis and his one-legged son, I've thought, What good are my blessings if they aren't also everyone's? And other times, I think, Who am I to say?

But for Philip's part: however hard he tries to remember the Gables time, it's fogged over, a dark passage, like he's the survivor of a traumatic twin birth. Aside from the mysterious fact that I came to visit him there every day, he remembers nothing.

The Chanteuse: 1994

WHAT DID RICHARD LEVITON know about his mother-in-law's past that didn't sound just like the story of her generation? She sang in beatnik coffeehouses a lifetime ago by the San Francisco Bay, and her beauty was in her misty, timid eyes. Her soprano voice was so opera-clear that even today, when it sailed forth in distress—"Oh! Oh!"—he could wonder if she was giving a staged reading of the line instead.

In her early twenties—when the glossy photo in Leviton's hand had been shot—she'd had a moonlike face framed by dark, frizzy waves and sang "Hey Lottie" holding the kind of full-bodied guitar that made everyone back then look like they were just starting lessons. He also thought he could see just a ghost of a future weight issue—that teeming, restrained quality that always looked to Leviton like the exact sell-by date of 1950s maidenhood.

Which probably wasn't the worst illusion for a coffee-house folk-singer to project: *Come away with me now. Never again a night like this.* During her prime, and for all purposes ending it, the boastful sculptor who would become her fiancé coaxed her to sail around the world with him in a suspiciously constructed midsized boat. And off she went, because something within her said she had to. Because he'd had the nerve to ask.

But by meeting his dare she seemed to wrest from him a reckless upper hand. The sculptor, who'd been a sickly boy, began showing signs of paranoia. He tried to prevent her singing in public. His possessiveness fed her martyrdom, and that talent people have for bringing about whatever catastrophe they fear the most, and in time he abandoned her with their two small children. Although it was she, Nola's mother, whom the world branded as unstable. This owing to her several nervous breakdowns, as they'd been called in those art-movie-house days.

Leviton replaced the photo in the dresser drawer.

Technically this wasn't snooping. Leviton had always assumed the role of placing the family mementos and hanging the art, while Nola's aptitude for decorating was more like her curls: either accidentally awesome or totally haywire, or both—just the kind of hard-knocked charm that Leviton secretly hoped he'd be inheriting through marriage.

Okay, now he was snooping. Counting on a few more seconds of languid afternoon to be AWOL from his wife and nursing son—it was New Year's Day, 1994—he fished out the contact sheet from that B movie in the Philippines. Definitely snooping. Nola, bare white breasts fluffed above a rumpled top sheet, a gardenia in her curls. Right leg hooking the famous male star's tattooed backside. Left hand prayerfully to his heart.

There'd been no actual penetration, Leviton knew. But he also knew the whole cast had been high as contrails, and that the tattooed male star, fully aroused, gave it a go: thrusting and suckling her lower lip, so that Nola had to stage-whisper as playfully as possible: *Cut*!

In fact, she'd alerted the director in his trailer, an act of boldness given her youth (19) and the era. Only to be laughed at: everyone knew the actor was *gay*. But that reassurance pacified Leviton even less than it did Nola. Hadn't she told Leviton that if he suckled her lower lip just so, she "couldn't turn back"? Was she reenacting that unconsummated scene? Was her whisper to the tattooed male star— with whom she remained friendly today—in the tone of no, or just *not now, not here*? There was no charming way for Leviton to voice his anxiety, so he filed the question for his prospective short-story cycle: *The Runowskis,* an interesting side project that he'd thought up on the second day of their honeymoon:

HUSBAND: an inventor-artist with an Edward Gorey mustache.

WIFE: his muse and secret brain.

GENIUS STROKE: In each installment, the final tableau would dissolve into an original canvas by the painter husband, redeeming into art whatever difficulty the adorably eccentric couple had just managed to transcend. The concept, Leviton felt, had all the markings of a publishing phenomenon. Possibly a cable series.

By contrast, he and Nola lost their adorability within minutes after the wedding—a civil ceremony so quirky she'd worn sneakers with bows, and even the justice of the peace got in on the photos. During the pregnancy (Nola's second, Leviton's first), she couldn't hold down any food but dried apricots. Her hair went flat, and a fibroid tumor outgrew the fetus, making intercourse too painful to try, only to shrink away as soon as Philip was born, its mischief fulfilled. To support her lower back, they ordered a god-ugly rose-patterned couch on sale—it sometimes made Leviton have to leave the room upon entering, and start his meditation over—and there was this new thing with her mouth, where her smile went up one side and down the other, a curse that was captured in every photo now, and Leviton felt certain he'd caused it.

Today it was mysterious side pain.

"Feeling any better?" he said, entering the living room.

Philip snoozed atop her, a nipple bobbing on his lip like the butt of a cigarette.

Nola's eyes were shut—until she seized up, like someone scorched by fire. "Sorry. I'm having a hard time. I'm having a really hard time."

"But what do you think's going on?"

"I don't *know*, Richard, maybe I should go to Kaiser. I mean, I would, if I could get a little help."

"It's not like I'm not right here to take you."

"Anyone can drive me. Not everyone can stay with your son," she said, and Leviton carried Philip to the crib in the boys' room, each step officially farther than his own dad had likely taken ever in his life.

A cheer went up from the house next door. Had the Rose Bowl begun?

"It's probably the worst day of the year to brave a waiting room!" Leviton called.

"Well, I still think we should dial the advice nurse. I guess you're already doing that. Obviously that's something you're going to do."

"You know they'll only say come in."

"I guess you know everything."

"Of course not. But you said it might be something you could walk off."

She was contorting herself upright, a rise to combat. Then she looked surprised to be standing.

"It's almost time to pick up Ronan at the Hendersons'," Leviton said, dipping his toe in that reality. "We could take a walk first, if you still want to. Or come lie down with me? Rest your eyes?"

She didn't soften, so he unhitched the padded stroller by the front door, his inner loneliness reaching tantrum pitch—a level of emotion, Leviton noted, that everyone in the family was allowed to express except him. What did that female counselor, the good one, say about Nola's walking away from intense discussions—*if you don't like how someone's banging on the door, how about answering it?*

How understanding that counselor had been! Although, admittedly, that made Leviton less sure about her actual credentials.

It took just a minute to wiggle the stroller across the threshold with Philip inside it, then to bump their way down the porch of their rented bungalow, and they were outside—the three of them, afoot, on New Year's Day in Long Beach.

To make a walk of it, he pointed them away from the Hendersons' driveway; away from the drunken Aussie husband and the laughing guests, who wore sarongs despite the absence of a pool. A dozen kids were shouting at once, all but the Hendersons', who ran

70

so impassively you didn't notice how blazing fast they were—the children of louts.

Through a picture window on Colorado Street, he tried stealing a glance at the Rose Bowl game while Nola limped behind. In movies, the whole charm of Nola's walk was the problem of her walk, breasts banging beneath a halter. Only now she seized up again. That hissing intake.

Leviton locked the stroller wheels and looked up to the sky, hearing Baby Philip honk out his greatest hits of near-speech, but when he looked down again, Nola had unlocked the wheels and was marching back the way they'd come.

"What are you doing?"

"I'm going to get a ride to urgent care. You're going to go get Ronan."

He thought of preventing her. What would protectiveness look like?

———

The Hendersons' party was becoming a yacht-rock songfest as Leviton buggied to their doorbell.

"Ronan!" called the wife, Lori, wagging a bottle of O'Doul's. "He'll pass this way if you stand still."

Behind them came a footrace of children doing laps through the house.

"I'll take this one," Leviton said, affecting a dad-chuckle.

But as soon as they'd buggied home, Nola was heading out, car keys jingling.

"I thought you couldn't drive."

"Just as far as my mom's. You know how slow she is getting dressed."

Leviton knew.

"I want to go with her!" Ronan said.

"Not this time," Leviton said. "We'll play K'nex."

"I want to go *with* her." Only repeat himself, and the world would understand.

"My sweetie! I'll be back!"

Then they were a men's retreat. As the evening proceeded from spinach tortellini to baths, as the Rose Bowl blared from the living room uncontested, Leviton read *Inspector Peckit* to both children—Philip rearing up in his crib while Ronan slurped his thumb, snuggling against Leviton, till the call came.

Naturally, it was a ruptured appendix. Naturally, she'd have died if they'd waited any longer. Were all doctors required to say this?

When the second call came, barely after 10 o'clock, she was already in recovery. Grace or good drugs had blanched her voice of vindictiveness, although this same calm brought home Leviton's predicament. Would she be days? Weeks?

Shamefully in the darkness of their bedroom, he let his worries reach, like infant hands, toward his writing career. A substitute worry, probably, but night after night he saved himself for it. Was this unique to men? Whatever hospital room Nola and her mother inhabited right now, they inhabited fully. Freed by their oppression. Freed from the need to prove anything to the world at all.

———————

Minutes or hours later, the siren of Philip's cry woke him.

The whooping intake, the shredding wail.

"You're going to love this," Leviton said, whipping up the unfairly addicting rice cereal. A bite for himself, a bite for Philip, who screamed his guts out again the instant he'd swallowed.

Wishing he had hips as he carried his son around the dark house, Leviton tried singing the heirloom of a lullaby that Nola had inherited from her family:

I gave my love a cherry / That had no stone
I gave my love a chicken / That had no bone
I gave my love a ring / That had no end

And found himself stirred by its prairie timelessness—the long human march of song-singing and tear-drying, a ring with no end, rolling forth to this very child . . . but after a few more rounds with Philip shrieking, Leviton had had enough timelessness.

"Do you hear this?" he whined into the phone to his AA sponsor, a vampiric musician who lived in Silver Lake. "I can't think. I can't meditate."

"*He's* your meditation now." It was the kind of utterly impractical genius that made Leviton miss the sponsor all the more.

Merely a transport vehicle to Nola, the padded stroller proved indispensable for its buckle restraints. With Philip strapped down, Leviton roamed the living room, stretched, returned to battle. At sunrise he parked the stroller outside the shower and stepped into a vast cosmos of relief. He woke his stepson (who, unlike Philip, seemed possibly high on the motherless adventure), tugged his feet through the cuffs of his jeans, and guided the stroller one-handed to the liquor store for crumb donuts.

Still, he was counting the days ahead. Was there a chance that his mother-in-law might take a shift? Holding a baby for photos, Carole often appeared to be tolerating a moment of discreet embarrassment. She would not tie children's shoes, apparently on principle. Leviton had discovered this pre-marriage, picking up Ronan for a surprise birthday party for Nola. Carole handed over the boy's lace-ups with equal parts fluster and windblown nonchalance. "I've never really done this," she said.

———

It was Day Three when Leviton called a domestic agency. "Unless you know a better way," he told Nola, "I can't spend more time away from my office."

She could nurse at this point, but she was forbidden to lift anything heavier than a newspaper, and she was walking like the rickety movie cowboy Walter Brennan.

"I guess you'll bring the kids with you, then. I guess you've figured something out."

"Oh stop that. Of course I have."

He was thinking of a married friend who, after arguing about housework, hired a maid for his half.

"And you're going to afford a nanny how? Take a second job, as a nanny?"

"If you think how much we'll lose if I can't work, it balances."

That very day, the agency sent Amparo—a Salvadoran of slightly less than middle age who pantomimed her questions about housework. Leviton hadn't known if it was politically incorrect to ask for an English speaker. "Like a doll!" she exploded upon Philip—the exact fawning comparison that the parents had often savored in private: Something Russian about the porcelain repose, the rouge of lips. The deal seemed clinched.

Next stop: the preschool, where Ronan was the late-arriving hero, survivor of a night with a stepdad whose skill had to do with writing things.

"I think Nola's sister is in your files?" Leviton told the aide. "For afternoon pickup?"

Bebe was the capable, golden-haired sister—inheriting their mother's soprano laugh but not the biting *ho ho ho*—and Leviton often felt she and he were Nola's earthbound protectors. Their mother's gene of stormy distrust skipped Bebe. Once, Leviton had questioned a book title on his mother-in-law's shelf, imagining it a gag.

"How to Win Every Argument?"

"Oh, ho," Carole said. "If you don't know how important that is, you will."

Back when Nola was dating every wrong guy before Leviton, she'd actually tried fixing him up with this practical sister—an unintended diss that thus had hurt him all the more. But only Nola could ever pierce him—the rude, wounded clown who'd been their sculptor father's favorite until he left.

It hit Leviton, stepping off the elevator to his rented office—it always hit him right about then—how little actual work he had to think about. *The Runowski Stories* had no patron. At a story lunch in Brentwood—a moonlighting opportunity—Leviton had dropped the name of Cody Castille, and the executive editor of *Zap* spun around in terror, as if alerted to the presence of a hit man. No assignment came of it.

Once, they'd welcomed him to report on the Middle American time-warp that was his new home in Long Beach—and only then, through the lens of legwork, did Leviton's surroundings start to fascinate him: The local pubs, into which off-duty hairdressers poked their heads to shout, *Anyone seen Tom?* The library clipping-file columns about "gals with pep" and "guys well up in fire department." The Soviet-seeming County Registrar's Office, where Leviton plied clerks with donuts and lattes to copy voting tables by zip code. It took three days to unlock a cherished factoid contrasting Ralph Nader-leaning precincts in Venice to Bob Dole precincts in Long Beach's Belmont Shore.

But he'd kept bringing his new marriage into the story, and it wasn't clear whether this was to feel superior to his new town or to celebrate it in a campy way—and they'd shelved it. Ever since, that editor didn't seem to look at him the same. Prozac, Leviton heard. He never should have brought up Cody Castille.

His lone assignment now was an article on second-generation hippie communes. But this involved little more than highlighting entries in The Directory of Intentional Communities for possible visits in spring, still months ahead. He moved to the futon and tried to digest, as research, *The Autobiography of Wavy Gravy.* A warm Santa Ana wind wafted in, and he wondered how you'd know if you were contracting Epstein-Barr. Hungry all at once, he got Chinese food across the street, then wandered Acres of Books, gathering an armful of monographs on Utopians.

At last, stretching things till 6, he drove home, but his mother in law's steel gray Pontiac blocked his space in the driveway. Not a power move, he told himself—she'd be tired after a day explaining Atticus Finch to highschoolers in South-Central. But did she have to?

"I was just leaving," she said in the kitchen, cupping her coffee mug with two hands, her operatic voice almost satirically obedient.

"Don't be ridiculous," Leviton said, taking Philip from the nanny for a few soulful nuzzles as Nola started more water to boil.

"You shouldn't be doing that," he said, meaning Carole should. "And isn't she here pretty late? I mean Amparo, not your mom."

Carole blew her daughter a meaningful kiss, rising to leave. She wasn't a hugger, but her goodbyes were always significant.

"Honestly?" said Nola. "I wouldn't know. Aren't you paying her the same either way?"

"I take to the park," the nanny said, placing Philip in the stroller and following Carole.

"Right. Though she'd probably like to get back to her own family."

"Well, you could assume that. But she seems to have a host of nanny friends at the park. *I'm* the one with no one to talk to."

Leviton looked at her. "Okay. I hear you loud and clear. But she likes Philip."

"Yup—she likes him a *lot*."

"Nola, is something wrong? I mean is something *new* wrong." That wasn't a good move.

"She calls him Perfect Baby. She knows the word *perfect*."

"Aren't you perfect, buddy?" Leviton called out to the porch. "It's a lot to live up to, I know."

"Why do I bother telling you anything, Richard? Believe me or just don't ask."

"Why do you have to be so reactive?"

"Because I'm tired? Can you tell I'm maybe just a little tired?"

Before the appendectomy (had it been years, now, or merely days?), when Nola was a song in her floral apron, Leviton enjoyed chasing his stepson, Ronan, around the backyard, wrestling on the grass. They'd come inside for dinner sweaty and adored by Nola and, the message went, weirdly virtuous just for being happy men.

But the stepson started adding to his repertoire a punishing knee-drop attack—sprung from a froggy headstand—and Leviton had accidentally encouraged this, releasing a giant "ooof!" the first time it landed. The higher the grownup tension in a room, the more likely

Ronan was to charge in and pounce.

"Not tonight," said Leviton, interrupting the frog maneuver. His tone was too jolly, so he had to capture the boy by the waist and lower him to the pillow just as Nola arrived to tuck him in.

"No books tonight," she murmured. "Too late for books." To Leviton, she cracked: "She's finally gone home—I mean *the nanny*." It was a rough kind of olive branch.

Philip lay conked on the sofa behind a berm of nursing blankets, a final puzzle piece to the day as Leviton closed shop. Already Nola had passed out on their bed.

Mere inches from spooning, Leviton could see, or make up seeing, her silhouette in cargo shorts. See how deftly they hung on her hips. He fantasized hippie hiker supplies in the pockets, baggies of dried ginger and weed. But he would not dare grind up against her, for the stitches—not to mention, now, the troubled air between them.

————————

From his office, a memory. Her foot out the window of his car as he drove.

Or was it the way that she never ignored a ringing phone, her willingness to suspend herself—to devote her full curiosity to the mystery of the present. As if she were French.

He phoned her now, to hear it again. That bewildered feminine sympathy.

"Hi?" she asked. Her openness reminded him of Ronan's long ago, greeting Leviton at the door as if a blindfold had just been wonderfully removed. As if the name Richard meant *"Are you the one we've waited for?"*

"What are you up to?" he began, easing himself onto his office futon.

"Oh, you know," she said, "important stuff. We're writing a window-shopping list of favorite foods. Your son hands me the crayons."

"That's actually brilliant."

"Things we'd require the staff to cook if we were elected president."

"That's important," he said. "You have to keep them learning new things, or they'll, they'll—mutiny? That's not the word."

"You don't ever want to be behind the scenes in a five-star kitchen for babies."

"How are they doing on the oatmeal? With the spoon catapults?"

They were laughing together!

All morning he'd been pleasantly back in it, his wonder at marrying Nola. The fact it was him and not, say, the gay tattooed costar.

When they were dating, she'd stalked Leviton with her camera and then tossed it to his bed, undressing him. She had that theater kid's flair for raunch. Tickling his armpit for a photo.

Leviton, of course, had been their straight man. The one with the degree in Poli Sci. Even in his failed acting days, with the Charlton Heston beard, he'd been an inhibited kind of actor. A contradiction in terms. Awkwardness was his only charm.

"I'm thinking of taking the holiday off," he said now.

"You should!" she said. "It's so nice."

He'd heard of his own father closing shop to woo his wife. That morning, in fact, after dropping Ronan, waving as the volunteers hung MLK projects from clothespins, Leviton had begun heading back toward home. It was some kind of whole-body Freudian slip.

In that first year of the Reverend King's holiday, the preschool co-op, feeling things out, voted to stay open for a fee. Why not capitalize on the childcare while they also had a nanny?

Never again a day like this, he thought, whipping the car around the corner to his street—until he saw Carole's steel gray Pontiac blocking the apron of the driveway. Well, it was her holiday, too.

Inside, Leviton held himself back. He caressed Nola's shoulders at the kitchen table. When the nanny returned with Philip from Cherry Park, he brought them a fresh T-shirt and matching visor, sending them back to the playground. When Bebe arrived with Ronan, his Barney t-shirt covered in fingerpaint ("Someone needs to bathe him," Carole sang. "That would be my guess"), Leviton hopped to the task. Crossing one more postponement off his list.

But while pouring water through a plastic windmill, he heard the front door slump shut. He wrapped his stepson in a towel and found

Nola's mother sitting with her coffee mug, alone.

"Where's Nola?"

Carole cleared her throat delicately. "She and Bebe went to relieve the nanny."

"So soon?"

"I believe Bebe said something about taking her to dinner. Because it's been so long since Nola's gone anywhere."

"Actually, I'd thought of doing something with her. While the nanny is still here."

"I guess that's between the two of you."

Leviton frowned.

She continued, almost faltering, "I should probably tell you that Nola's car got a street cleaning ticket last week. It's going to get another ticket at 7 a.m. if you don't—you know."

"Right."

"I guess you'll need to move it to the other side of the street. Or come and drive it away."

"When I can get a ride. I'd need a ride over to do that."

"Well, you could get one tonight. But I guess you have important things to do."

"Yeah. I mean I'd rather not tonight."

"But you're working on it?"

"We'll see," Leviton said.

"We'll see?"

"Or, Carole, I'll pay a parking ticket."

She gave an amazed laugh.

"Carole, it's not practical for me to come two hours before the pre-school opens. How about if l fetch you the key. Then you can move her car."

"You don't need to 'fetch' anything. The key is already in my house."

"Then why haven't you moved the car?"

"I was afraid of this exactly," Carole said, palms down on the table. "That this would become my concern."

"That's exactly what none of this is. Your concern."

"You kids don't have the *money* to pay tickets. While you pretend you can pay for a nanny. She grades my papers for extra food money. Have you noticed her health?"

"I need to do some things now."

"I'll be off. Just as soon as I finish this cup."

"I'll take the cup." Out of body, he took her cup. "Next time, I'd really love it if you didn't park in the driveway. I like to think about that, sometimes, while I'm carrying two kids up the block to my car."

"Oh," she said. "Oh!"

"You did what?" Nola was asking him, minutes later.

"I'm sorry! I'll call her as soon as she gets home!"

"I feed," Amparo said, enacting a contest over who should spoon out Philip's dinner.

Leviton stepped in to feed his son. Though of course things were screwed beyond recognition now.

"I'm just calling to make amends," he recited into the phone the next morning. "For becoming heated. I would also like to take responsibility, Carole, for my part in the whole breakdown over the car. I've come to see—"

"Oh, your phony maturity. Your oh-so-spiritual remorse."

———————

"What did she say?" Nola asked.

For once Leviton knew not to answer. The next night would be his AA meeting. Even, or especially, in times of conflict, Nola would be forced to indulge him that.

A buddy to help retrieve Nola's car. Bebe to help with Philip. He envied Nola's family network, though of course it was hard to complain when he was the beneficiary of it.

It was near the Chavez offramp, hurtling northbound on the 101, that Leviton remembered, like a cry in search of a throat, how badly he'd come to miss metropolitan LA. By gradients of neutral, forsaken light, his frustrations began to feel smaller and more humorous—his was the tale of one more misfit in a city of misfits.

He beheld the outcroppings of stunted highrises to the left, the earthquake traps to his right, ivy climbing their flanks—in the spaces between which sat the stucco ruin of a building he felt he'd never seen.

It bore, in a tagger's scrawl, his own name. In possessive case. *Richard Leviton's.*

By then, of course, he'd shot past, and was threading the downtown cloverleaf. Nor was there hope of circling around and glancing twice.

Asking his racing heart to take a moment, he tried some homely explanations. Once, for example, he'd read in the *Los Angeles Times* about a slumlord who shared his name.

Although, if he were honest, the answer that appealed to him more was that somewhere in the barrio—where it was conceivable that a handful of hipsters or ghetto nerds read a music magazine to which Leviton contributed—he had a fan. A cholo fan, maybe an ironic, self-styled group of them. Their journalism teacher, a visionary with a passion for developing minority voices, could have distributed one of Leviton's stories in class. Leviton might even prefer not to know the truth, for the pleasure of pondering the question.

Arriving to the safety of the meeting hall—a carpeted midsized auditorium on a hill atop Chinatown—he took a seat in the third row and exhaled. This tribe that asked nothing of him to belong. Had he known it was so simple—had he known *he* was so simple—he might never have drank. But he couldn't have belonged *until* he'd drank. A circular riddle. A koan.

It came to him he had a son. A wife and son!

He felt like a beggar, trying on a velvet robe.

Even if the graffiti referenced, for public shaming, a slumlord with Leviton's name, that prospect offered its own genealogical intrigue. Who were these Leviton slumlords, these magnates with the business sense he'd lacked?

"So, you know how Jerry Lewis is a superstar in France?" he said to Nola on his return, bursting to share what he'd seen.

"We can't have Amparo anymore," she began in the dark living room.

"We—what?"

"She warned me that she's going to kidnap Philip."

81

Leviton commanded his eyes not to roll.

"Besides, I'm ready to lift things. Maybe."

Enough street light shone in for Leviton to see her seize up, the sudden grimace, as if for old time's sake.

"How can I get you to back up a minute?"

"I can probably handle things, Richard."

"The doctor said you're supposed to feel sure."

"Then someone else has to do it."

"Look," Leviton said. "Did she maybe say, I could just kidnap you, my nino! I could eat you up!"

"Oh, ho. Good try."

"But what did she say? What actual words?"

"Don't you interrogate me."

"I just mean, you know, what if you're projecting? You're in a vulnerable place, which reminds you of your childhood, and—"

"She described a nature show on TV. She kept saying, 'The ape take the baby.' The ape. Takes. The baby. Got it?"

"She's the ape?"

"Clearly *you'd* never have such a thought."

"If she's the ape, why would she warn you?"

"Because that's what criminals do. Or she could be rubbing it in. That we're, you know, the colonialists. The imperialists?"

Leviton floundered. "But doesn't this all sound a little, I don't know—Marxist? For a woman who watches telenovelas? And why would she call herself an ape?"

"I don't know! To make it proud. Like rappers with the n-word."

"Oh, for Christ's sake."

"I'm strong enough now," she repeated. "I think so, anyway. But who knows."

"Oh, well!" he said. "Who knows! You're *probably* fine!" Two could sound like idiots.

———

Nanny-less, they staggered to spring, which was when Nola's

grandmother on her father's side—long estranged but indelible, a giver of art lessons, a brassy role model—died in Santa Clarita. It mattered to Nola not only that they attend the funeral but stay the day. "Since your flight isn't till Monday," she added as they drove.

"Here it comes," Leviton said. "You're barely looking."

Past the tenements, it loomed. Like an iceberg, like a barge.

"Now! You're not looking!"

"At what?"

"At what! I'm pulling off."

Being on surface streets, however, only compounded the difficulty of finding a specific, graffitied wall. Leviton was lucky to find his way back to an onramp, luckier still that it was sufficiently south-ward to afford them a second pass. "There will be a brick building with a fire escape," he whispered, as though they were storming the place. "And the beige wall is alongside it. But it's going to come fast."

"Where alongside?"

"Directly alongside."

"I think you should keep your eyes on the road!"

"And I will. If you will just keep your eyes on the house. There! You see it?"

"No."

"Then you need glasses."

"It's not there."

"You have to be trying to miss it. It was painted to be seen. You don't paint a sign by a freeway to make it hard to see."

"Drop it. I don't like your intensity right now." She read his eyes. "And do not bring up that therapist."

"My voice rose, Nola, because of the urgency. Because it was going by in a flash."

"There was nothing there."

"The person who doesn't see something doesn't get to say it isn't there."

"Remember that," she said. "Remember that one."

A large Coca Cola truck steamed ahead of them, then fell behind.

Leviton sighed, shifting his troubled mind to the commune

itinerary. There would be two days in Sacramento with the "Alphabet Threat" collective, one night in San Francisco for a squatter house concert followed by the breakfast interview with Wavy Gravy. Then the Sierras, where a girl named Moondance—whose voice on the phone from a sandal shop had evoked buzzing bees and innocence and figs—and a certain casual, sensual freedom—and an annoying note of therapeutic concern—would introduce Leviton to the rest of her tribe.

Details which, could he share them with Nola, might reawaken her onetime eco-idealistic Buckminster Fuller high-school-intellectual . . . joie de vivre? The place where their eccentric dreams once touched. It had been her idea in the first place, that he do a story on modern communes!

"It's really necessary we stay all day?" he whined. "I still have to pack."

"Kind of," she said.

Of course he knew why. Here on the springy bed of the Santa Clarita Great Western—as if it were some other daughter he'd left—here was Nola's father, the sculptor, planting wet, loud raspberries on Philip's belly, over and over, to the baby's shocked delight—Leviton almost rose from his chair to intervene.

It was not till after the burial, together in one car, that her father dipped a toe into the past. "You'll think I don't mean it, but I hope you'll give your mother my regards. She wasn't strong enough to make it?"

Nola didn't answer.

"She's the same, then?" her father cackled.

"The same as when I was three?" Nola came off as merely parrying. "What could be the same?"

"Forget it. I was trying to make it easy for you to share with someone who'd understand."

"Dad, I won't even presume to understand what triggered the two of you. I know we all have our quirks."

In the back seat, Leviton tried to appear pleasantly deaf, gazing at his own reflection in the rearview.

"So you know," the sculptor went on, "the court system back then, the whole therapeutic community, was telling fathers to move on. I could have fought. I could have brought up your mother's boyfriends. Would that have been good?"

"The philosophy was not sending cards on birthdays?"

"If I was going to put things behind me, no." He looked somber. And then, for some reason, shocked. "God, you must be making your husband uncomfortable! Richard, forgive us."

"No, no!" Leviton said, "I'm just glad you guys are talking. I know it's a sad day for you both."

What, by marrying this woman, had he pushed his way into? Leviton considered just the fallout that he'd known of. Her "relationship" with her high-school teacher. Her radar for creeps and predators. Had the nanny really planned something?

Her father talked about a new exercise routine, his promotions at the local college, details flung back through the car by the wind through the open window. Until they'd rolled up to the gravel motel lot. "That's the deal. I'm going to be cleaning out my mom's trailer for another week or so. Before I leave." He undid the electronic locks. "That's the deal, I suppose."

It looked like the world's most passive invitation.

"We'll have lunch!" Nola said, landing a sock on her father's shoulder, turning things campy.

"I have a lot to do, like I said. But if you call me at Grandma's trailer, we could set a day." He turned to face the infant car seat. "Will you look at that sleeping little czar. Is there Russian on your family tree, Richard?"

"The whole tree, basically," Leviton said—but this elicited a lecture about the Russian avant-gardist Kazimir Malevich.

There followed a quiet return to Long Beach—followed, two days later, by Leviton's flight and then a drive to the center of the mind's eye, somewhere in the northern Sierras. A crushed pastel road hurtling into a mine shaft of leaves, tires grinding up sage and mesquite and a compost of ancient figs; and then, in a bit of ludicrous staging, the rental car skidding right up to the naked Moondance, seated on a blanket with a naked bearded teenage boy named Dylan.

Here they were, where life began.

And yet—throughout the hippie prayer circles, and the home-made millet crusts being fed hand-to-neighbor's mouth, throughout the tours of the swimming holes and the geodesic yurts—what Leviton felt most sharply as a reporter was a kind of traveler's guilt.

A duffel over each shoulder upon his return to LAX. A trio of phones by a janitorial closet, two pay calls to their answering machine. No sign of Nola and the kids.

On the long Super Shuttle ride home, the sun switched windows, roasting his legs. They had to drop a passenger in Redondo Beach and another at the Long Beach Hyatt. His back ached now. He should have peed.

When he stepped off the van before their little bungalow, Nola was rounding the corner in fast, banging steps, while Philip lifted himself against the stroller restraints with his voyager's gaze cast forward. "Da!" he clucked. "Da!"

"There's your hero," Nola said. "There's Da."

"You're angry with me?" Leviton said.

She said nothing.

"I'm the one who got stranded at the airport"—and all at once, Leviton was not sure if what he needed was to pee or eat or sit. He was dizzy. A school of starfish was devouring the pressure point behind one ear.

"We got there barely twenty minutes late, Richard! There was an accident!"

Not only could Leviton not argue his case, he couldn't remember it. "You still got back ahead of me. My gosh, Nola, I need to lie down."

"I'm getting the house ready for my dad," she said as they headed in. "You said you'd help."

"In the morning," he winced. "Tomorrow I'll help."

"You—!" she began, but curtailed, whirling toward the kitchen.

Leviton had dropped both bags beside the ugly couch, where, as if it were the sanest idea he'd ever had, he slid to the floor, lowering his neck and back onto one of the duffels. That was when Ronan charged from his room.

He would have bet he had no reflexes at all. But before Ronan's Vans could stick their landing onto Leviton's crotch, Leviton's knees snapped shut and recoiled, sliding the boy back-first into the sofa's wooden leg.

"Jesus!" Leviton moaned, cupping Ronan's head as the boy wailed.

Nola flew to the room, eyes accusing.

Dialing his sponsor in Silver Lake, holding the phone at the end of its long cord, he closed the bedroom door, but it flew open with a bang, making him jump, humiliating him besides—a vacuum cleaner behind it. "Incredible," she said. Then she left him in darkness, delirious, wishing for her pity. His dreams involved stationary bicycles in tropical rainforests.

When daylight came, he begged, "There's no way I can socialize. Please. Have lunch with him at a restaurant."

"Are you doing this on purpose?"

But she let Leviton have his way, leading the children outdoors, leaving Leviton a shaming the size of a house.

A fever song, in the form of a round, began transmitting from a device behind Leviton's ribcage; he discovered it could be muted slightly by drinking pitchers of ice water. The water treatment was also imperative in order to save a darting gazelle with the head of Nola from a terrifying ape with the head of the nanny, so long as his rival, Tarzan, a tattooed actor with ill intent, did not arrive first to the rescue.

Then the fever song was only another doorbell and his name being shouted in anger.

Ronan entered first, cavorting. Then Philip, squirming on Nola's shoulder as she attempted to sing him back asleep.

"I had to lay him down on the porch to let myself in," she said. "Thanks so much for locking the door."

"I. Am. Sick," Leviton lectured, and it was his own father speaking. "And he likes you to sing louder. He falls asleep to loud music in the car."

"No one needs your bullshit unless you're going to take care of him."

"I'm going to start by explaining how not to talk to me." Not words he'd have picked on his best day. But they felt suddenly like the wellspring of life. "Wait. How was lunch with your father?"

She slammed the boys' door from within, setting the lock, as Ronan sometimes did, while Leviton, as he sometimes did, retrieved the screwdriver they kept for just that purpose.

He waited ten minutes before rapping calmly, perhaps eerily, with one knuckle. "You'll need heat. It's going to get cold." He felt shockingly whole. "I'm opening this door and letting heat in."

TABLEAU of an open room. Mother and children, dredged, theatrically he felt, to the farthest corner of Ronan's bed. Leviton standing before them, a sad, noble guardian with a screwdriver. "You needed heat!" he said.

———————

Even in divorce, in their unsold television series, the Runowskis would share as many charming memories as bad ones—largely on account of the on-screen minutes they spent smiling over the developmental quirks of their children.

For example, their youngest son never mastering the crawling phase.

Rather than hands and knees across the carpet, he zigzagged, like a gondolier, arms first to one side and then the other—a prelude to the jaunty, lopsided toddle that the family thought looked irrepressible instead of medically concerning.

Look at Nola in twenty years, her curls as faded as driftwood. It seems to Leviton she never got over that postoperative, Walter Brennan limp. She does not remember the rowing.

His mother-in-law lives on too, misty and wise.

The morning after his return from the Sierras, delirious with fever, Leviton stood with phone in hand, ready to confront the former nanny for sabotaging his marriage. But which number to call? The agency? The therapist? Buckminster Fuller?

Instead he would attempt to reclaim the pieces of his young family. But how to convince Carole—who sounded like an apologetic hostage—to bring Nola to the phone?

Like an abductee, he marched himself to the car, meeting-bound. Halfway to Chinatown, he slowed. Then accelerated. Then veered to the Chavez offramp. Block by block, in the waning LA light, Leviton searched for the tenement that bore his name.

He could still see the uncharted space within that phone call, and farther back Philip—nervously clucking, navigating the vast, carpeted ocean of Carole's living room. "Oh, you kids tried, didn't you," she said, "you really tried." The lamentation seemed so old-fashioned that, in 1994, Leviton would have sworn that it was sarcasm.

New Journalism: 1995

"Should we go down to the water?" Richard Leviton said, already veering from the boardwalk, and Bailey Kavanagh—he didn't need to see her follow because he could feel her behind his shoulder—answered, "I don't have anywhere else to be."

It was May 1995, and he could count a few hours before his magazine writing group at Extension, tonight starring guest speaker Bailey. Out of character for Leviton, but egged on by her gaze, he peeled the flapping shirt off over his head. It was a lush green paisley that made him think, the way a photo in a locket might, of flower children in the 1960s. Then he undid his Levi's with the waistband of his trunks shining beneath. Virtually no one able to read health warnings in English swam at Venice Beach anymore, but he could swear he'd seen a newscast that said certain critical fish (bellwether fish? trendsetter fish?) were returning, and, anyway, all the sensory pleasures of the boardwalk seemed to cut him loose from worry. The jangled plop of his jeans to the sand, the smell of gin and fries.

"Just like that?! You're going in?"

He looked at her. She hid her size, as always, behind a men's dress shirt that reached to the knees of her black leggings. An invisible purse held before her in both hands. Sovereign. A bystander. Yet she lived for writing that risked everything, tried to capture everything.

She was a vicarious sensualist, if that made sense.

The sun was hovering like a lost ball over deeper water and Leviton strove toward it. He turned back once to see that Bailey was watching, but then, suddenly, a field of shadow from a cloud raced across the surface of the water, like a magician's tablecloth, and for a flash he felt utterly alone—as if her attention held no actual concern for him, or for anything. Just random attention. But something about that, too, made him feel adult and brave.

A first real wave broke, and Leviton porpoised under it. The cold encased him, erased all inner argument, and when he surfaced, a second, larger wave had arrived, which he rode almost all the way to shore. He rode two more, but his ears began to ache, so he headed in.

"The person who looks the most out of place on sand," he panted, rubbing the shirt against his wet face. "I drifted south a ways, but it was easy to find you."

"Everything's so much bigger than I remember it!" she said. "Bigger, but less *vast*."

"Yeah? I remember going to Cape Cod once." Leviton felt his words bang mute against the towel as he lay his head down. "And thinking, if you live there and you're facing east, and the sun keeps backing away from you all day long, does it make you feel left behind by the rest of the country? I mean in some subliminal way?"

"I promise no one there has ever given it a thought. Where the sun goes next."

"No? You always say the brainpower in DC is so intoxicating."

"It is! But LA has all the surprises. All the amazing light. And stories *everywhere*."

"Oh, good. My class needs to hear that."

Actually, Leviton wasn't sure. Editors often hated his notion of a story idea. Once, with Bailey's blessing, he'd profiled one of his buddies: a divorced dad, now car-less, roaming Long Beach with a backpack and Big Gulp and a book of Chekhov. The closing image had evoked. . .celestial conveyance? The journey to life's end, in the form of his vagabond buddy trudging a suburban block.

"Are you still bummed being back at the Weekly?" he asked.

"I can't even talk about it. Hate, hate, hate. It's the first time I've ever been the odd man out."

"I can't picture that at all."

"In meetings now, when Kevin dislikes an idea, he'll say, 'Ah, nope.' As if he'd wished he could be more tactful. And then Felicia laughs like a teenager."

Leviton nodded slowly. "I may have glimpsed some of that. When I offered to review the Sandy Koufax biography—"

"I heard about it. He said you needed to query in writing."

"He *told* you?"

"Will you forget him? Please? He got Salman Rushdie to respond to a bedside reading questionnaire, and now he thinks Nobel Prize winners are going to audition for the *LA Weekly*."

"Kevin's always had a little chip on his shoulder, I guess. Some agent in Manhattan asked him, 'Are there good LA novelists, or is it all detective stuff?'"

"He loves that story." Bailey brushed sand off her leggings. "Regardless, keep submitting."

"Who said anything about stopping? I'll send some things."

"Thank you. Selfishly speaking, please do."

"Selfishly? You're saying they don't *like* me?"

"I'm saying they don't like *me*."

Leviton felt a measure of unchivalrous relief. Followed, right afterwards, by a premonition of concern on Bailey's behalf. She'd been the epitome of cutting edge just a decade ago—the house mascot, the magic punk. "I still say Koufax was too perfect a subject to query about."

Bailey was shaking her head. "No, Kevin's right."

"But you agreed he was being absurd!"

"Because it was you," she announced. "*You* should never need to query a story. For anyone." The more over the top her praise, the more it seemed to convince her.

Leviton checked his watch. "We'd better go."

They had to hotfoot around a guy skating backward on the boardwalk, then lean against the rail of a grimy bar patio so Leviton could dress—the same patio where, on New Year's Day in 1981, he'd watched UCLA race out ahead of Illinois on the way to a rout. Was there an essay in this? A sunset story on the death of beach culture, how the California idea once held the nation's breath. "Beauty whose fair flower, being once displayed, doth fall that very hour…."

"I can't get over how adorable you and Philip were," she said now as he spread the sandy towels onto the car seats.

She had been in good Bailey form at Farmers' Market—admiring Leviton's two-year-old son while at arm's length, both entertained and struck dumb by the existence of such a creature. There was a subject for a writer: Fathers' rights. Ah, nope. He didn't need Kevin Claire to decide that. Let alone Nola, Leviton's ex.

The drive to UCLA, he must have forgotten, would prove tortuous, from Lincoln Boulevard, soon to be gentrified but presently lined by clapboarded Hoagie huts, over to ghostly Pacific Ocean Park, where roller coasters used to tip you toward the sea. Then the new deco hotels of Santa Monica, their cafes brassy and gleaming as the sky darkened, reminding him he'd better rescind the promise of a meal before class.

Bailey merely shrugged, settling for a cup of vending machine broth on the walk from the parking structure (when did large women do all that eating?).

She toted the steaming cup inside the classroom door, and Leviton stationed or maybe stranded her beside the pulldown screen in the front of the room while he retreated to the back, booting up the overhead projector. *This can't be the immortal* Washington Post *woman*—so he imagined them all thinking.

It hit him: bring her a chair.

"Hi!" She waved to the group, as if waiting for someone to waterbomb her.

———————

Which also lets some of the air out of his scripted introduction, but he pushes ahead, in a voice that he hopes has found the sweet spot between actual reverence and hammy, ironic reverence. He invokes that pantheon of editing gods whose names are so imposing they begin to sound made up—Graydon Carter, Ben Bradlee, Anna Wintour. On a less celebrated tier ("They're that good," Leviton adds), but arguably more vital, are those daring talents known as "writer's editors"—angels, essentially, inhabiting two realms at once, performing that miraculous feat of keeping commerce on speaking terms with art. And no such figure, to a growing list of writers on both coasts, is held in any higher esteem than this woman sitting before you: Bailey Kavanagh.

But first—having the great fortune to have worked with her himself—he feels he must attest to the many roles that an editor like Bailey Kavanagh must play. Champion, muse, lifesaver, risk-taker. Sounding board at 3:00 am. Job functions, Leviton confesses, that writers on assignment all but took for granted, once upon a time, back, say, in the 1970s, when it seemed that all of his own literary heroes—Cody Castille, Charlie Haas, Rian Malan—were writers whom Bailey Kavanagh edited. (The names mean zilch to Leviton's students, but the silence, perhaps, passes as awe-filled.) Bylines, brilliant at the very border of what could have been unprintable, that a fellow artist always spots with either envy or reawakened hope. For god's sake, how long has he been talking?

"We're kind of playing wow the editor," he explains to Bailey, beaming a queue of student submissions onto the wall above her head. There's a screen, but no one can seem to reach the pull ring, until Camille Davison, with a competence bordering on anger, hooks it with the stiletto heel of her strappy boot. Applause. "So basically, chime in with any feedback you've got."

One by one, of course, the proposals hurt his eyes. There is a PR-inflected review of a chain restaurant, which Leviton tries to refashion as a Zeitgeist piece. Stacy Alvarez offers readers a "ringside seat at a boxing ring," and Leviton, already dumbed down, can't seem to articulate what's less than poetically precise about a metaphor attached to the same thing as itself.

Bailey tells a young woman (Vianney, is it? He always confuses her

94

with the other magenta-haired one) that a story about the campus's new study lab might benefit from the writer's own moody, first-person presence. Or else try a connoisseur's take: What makes for the quintessential study space? Is it the right tree outside the window? The artificial light?

The student looks accused, or concerned for Bailey's sanity. "It's more kind of—regular."

When Hannah Lopate pitches a phone interview with the young founder of an "online diary" called Links.net (which "just might" offer a new paradigm of self-expression), Leviton is barely listening. "Wouldn't he matter only to readers who hang out on the Web?" he hears himself say.

"And? Those are the readers of the future," Ms. Lopate says, and Leviton prays that his embarrassment doesn't show. "Good! Put that in the query, then."

In the waning minutes, David Bornstein—a favorite of Leviton's—proposes, for *GQ*, the witty journal of a week spent growing the soul patch on his lower lip. Would it change his life? Would he shoot billiards with Luke Perry?

"Why the suspense?" Leviton coaxes. "Tell us what happened!"

But Bornstein's answer drifts into the weeds. First his girlfriend, Bess, complained that the whiskers tickled. ("Where?" teases Stacy Alvarez. A chorus of scandalized howls.) The couple had a fight over something trivial, and the girlfriend moved out mid-week. Why? Bornstein is unclear on the journalistic ethics of phoning to ask her. Where does reporting end and life begin? He's having a lot of feelings—complicated feelings.

Leviton is speechless, of course, enrapt, because what he hears is an ending worthy of O. Henry. A soul-patch experiment conferring. . . *soulfulness*. The earnest young writer at his shaving mirror, initiated to the world of love and loss.

Did anyone else see? Would Leviton himself—a newly divorced father, suddenly nearing forty—ever again have space to dream like a writer? It had happened so quickly, this passing of the torch.

He stands fingering the sandy waistband beneath his jeans until

Bailey saves him. "Keep in mind, they'll probably want you to have a track record first, unless you're offering a finished piece, on spec. And even then, at the majors. . . ?"

A sad silence follows.

"I hope I haven't been too realistic," she says.

Adorable.

They don't escape right away, however. As Leviton escorts his guest from the hall, Camille Davison, the stilettoed one, blocks his path—accidentally, Leviton assumes. Till it isn't that.

Even without using fashion heels to grab movie screens, the student has sometimes unnerved him. Her stance is always the same combination of jeopardy and rapt defiance, fight and flight. A vaguely disturbed young type, Leviton has made up: A hater (and needer) of men, chained to a wheel that goes round and round. *Avoid!* his instinct always says—while also, even now, luring him, hard, as if he lost something behind her ear. Suddenly he remembers: an emailed essay.

"You couldn't read it?"

"Shoot! Did I not reply? I remember thinking it was good!"

Ms. Davison smirks, nodding, and her eyes have welled with righteous tears. "Okay, you know what that was? That was shitty of you. The contest deadline was midnight."

The "shitty" remark hangs there. If its overfamiliarity were less outrageous, Leviton would have no problem calling it out. Instead it embraces him, pools up inside like the nerve-sharpening potion of his breakdowns with Nola, when all was on the line—he could never distinguish, it seems, a woman's accusation from the magical prospect that she might care.

"I'm truly sorry," he says, "I am, but there's not always time to reply to students' emails. It's even on the syllabus."

"Wow," she says as she turns to leave. "Wow," separately, to Bailey.

It's safe to say Bailey is puzzled, although not nearly so shaken as Leviton, whose walk toward the parking structure repeatedly stops and starts.

"Are you okay?" she asks.

Honestly? He isn't. The whole day has stranded him on a thin, unsteady ledge. Kevin Claire hates him; he self-importantly raised a student's hopes and dashed them; he bored them all with tales of the 1970s. He is depressed—ever depressed. He's the White Male Author the whole world has begun to see through.

"You were too kind," Bailey says. "To all of them. Seriously."

"No, you're the one being kind."

He lobs his valise into the backseat, then comes around to open the door of his long-ago, one-night clumsy lover, toying solemnly with the question of whether he all along ought to have loved Bailey. In the anode light of the roof level parking, they hover—every time they hang out, he ends up hovering.

But his confidence, it's been punctured. And, of course, her weight. He never could quite get around her weight.

It's possible, here on the West Side, he smells the ocean, or is it her hair? He touches it, as if the gesture might feel more like himself.

"Not fair," she complains. Then: "Really?" Exactly as she'd asked ten years ago.

Their lips brush, then part. He is already aware how her shape will feel, behind the kiss—her body to him is a strange, almost planetary abstraction, no edge or flaw or incompletion or question on its surface—and, it's a shameful fact about him—he can't.

"I don't understand you," she says, buckling in.

"I know it."

"All those years I watched you fall for the dramatic ones. You went for idiots! Psychopaths! While I swooned for you."

Leviton gets in behind the wheel. The moment for kissing has gone. "That's a cool shirt," he segues, or fails to.

"It would be perfect for you! Take it."

He stops himself from lifting a playful eyebrow.

"Seriously, when you drop me off. I've got a dozen of them I'm getting rid of."

"Why on earth?"

"If you don't like them, they're for Goodwill. I have a whole pile of vintage Towncraft. Peaches and limes. Men's camp shirts."

"But why don't you want them?"

"I don't know. I don't even know why I wore this. Maybe because it's old-timey."

"Like me."

"Not like you. I'm just done with that look. It's been building."

"If you're sure," he says, and they both look elsewhere at the same time. She seems to want him to say more, so he does. "I'm too tired to debrief, I guess. But seriously, I'm glad you're back."

"Oh, stop," she says, and that's that.

"Wishing, when we were all so young, that I could have been as complicated as one of his characters"—she'd actually written those words, in the recommendation letter that got him this teaching gig. Always tempting him to believe that his innate flaws might really be his greatest virtue... And whenever he'd written as though this were the case, when he risked more truth on the page than he actually thought sane, he could count on her famous exclamations in the margins, which sped directly to his brain.

Up floats a memory from 1985. (On the hour's drive to Long Beach, there is going to be time for lots of memories.) Leviton, newly sober—breaking tortilla chips in a bowl of guacamole. Bailey, loitering by the back stairs, a crasher at her own bon voyage. Which, to be honest, feels less a going-away than some sad kind of auction, like she's waiting for someone (himself?) to place a bid.

One of her guests calling for a speech, which she refuses. Nobody could refuse a request as serenely as Bailey.

She'd assigned him one last piece, a participatory feature about a gathering of daredevil glider pilots outside Reno ("If there were time, we'd look for someone macho"). When Leviton's AA group didn't forbid him, as he prayed they would, he packed his brand new Big Book and went. Intimidated to his core, colliding again and again—not mid-air, thank god—with the squat billionaire sponsor, the Caesar-cut hotelier in the Members Only windbreaker, Leviton did what his journalistic heroes had always done: captured the powerful man

98

of action looking dumb.

But when she left for DC, he started to spiral. He pissed away a plum column at the Weekly. His subjects, in succession, were: the ineffable sadness of Bel Air swimming pools (they proved, literally, ineffable); a comedy traffic school with an unfunny instructor; a late-night host whose show taped self-deprecatingly in the Valley to take advantage of the low-watt locale. (Leviton fled the set to depict a rune-like nest of welcome signs on the meridian of Van Nuys Boulevard that used to creepify him as a child. Kiwanis, Masons, a vanished race of ancestors.)

"I should go back to features," he told Cody Castille, during one of the garrulous rock critic's afternoon drop-ins. In Leviton's hothouse Koreatown apartment, where he holed up with the Big Book and a pilfered Russ Myers VHS—the one his roommate owned for campiness but which Leviton recognized as a Trojan horse for porn—Cody had hoped to complain about his gaspingly lovely painter girlfriend, Dehlia, as if Leviton could even hear her name without unmooring like a bouquet of balloons.

Cody was perplexed by defeat in any form. "It's called columnist's disease, man. It passes. No one quits a column."

But in these words, Leviton heard hope of a greater distinction. And quit the column.

Bailey still wrote to him, raving in her chunky cursive about her life at *The Post*. About 25-year-old Pulitzer nominees, matinees of *Footloose*, and the power-chord Pixies, whose girl vocalist singing "Gigantic" sounded like she was holding Godzilla in one hand and a sex toy in the other. Whole postcards on the subject of nightclub sweat.

But Bailey had been only the soundtrack, never the subject, of Leviton's romantic dreams.

It was true: He'd fallen, again and again, for the dramatic ones.

After Sylvie, the one from Boston, there'd been a 22-year-old rock critic, Dell (whose name Leviton tried to construe as the junior reader's edition of Dehlia).

"How would you like a blind date with a runaway?" Cody had suggested one day.

"Upper-case runaway? Or lower?"

She arrived an hour late cursing about her boss; during sex, she posed like a WWII pinup, but punk, with smoky eye—a hollow routine that felt, paradoxically, reserved for a special, kind someone.

Within days they were crashing at her place, behind the Capitol tower, even more of a hamper than Leviton lived in, while Dell's roommate, an MTV "veejay," entertained a series of touring rock stars in the next room. Sober, Leviton imbibed the mossy delights of the Hollywood underground.

One night, she left him waiting so long after a Beastie Boys release party that he blubbered to his AA sponsor, who labeled her an *arrested adolescent*—a term Leviton recognized as ammunition. When he repeated it to Dell, shaking a paternal finger, she threw a shot glass that whistled past his ear, exploding against the wall.

Bailey, visiting town over the holidays, was unimpressed. They'd all three gone for Mexican food, and Bailey barely talked, complaining of jet lag, four days in.

The punch line, Leviton realizes now, is how few months it took for stability to turn Dell into the couple's dowdy, practical half—the one with the skin creams and the NPR tote bag. Somehow he'd released her inner coupon-clipper. She went macrobiotic, applied to law school at Bolt. They barely had sex. She pressured him to get a real career.

That was about the time, needing a painter's lowdown for a story about a local art academy, that he'd gone to visit Dehlia.

He'd already heard Cody's side of their breakup (the broken tape recorder, her ludicrous denial), now he heard hers ("His tone was extremely condescending! As if I were a child! A very bad child!").

She stood quaking with understudy autonomy, skimming a net through a pool at a housesitting gig in Pasadena, and Leviton could not tell if a hand on her shoulder would be chivalry or the absolute opposite. In a neon two-piece, her skin had been so freshly toweled

100

and dusky no guy could have stood too long a look (the raised dots between lanes, just now, tell him he's swerving). Pairing up felt so wrong as to be inevitable.

For a tragic flower, it turned out, Dehlia took a rather dominating role in goofing off. There'd been her zany style dancing to Kool and the Gang—miming every instrument, striking the imaginary high hat and, each time, voicing it (*Ding!*). And there was her Transylvanian professorial purr—"*This is not good, Richard,*" she would frown, inspecting an expired carton of eggs.

She installed herself naked, a flipped beetle, on his bed, cooing while he typed away on deadline, her scrubbed face translucent and vaguely ill.

At the same time, she was worldlier than Leviton, and possessed more bohemian gifts. Those smooth yet calloused hands, hammering picture frames. Her tastes, the famous names she dropped. He might draw her close, fumbling for advantage, but before they could kiss, she would step back and rearrange his hair. It was all Leviton could do not to bat away her hand.

Equally troubling, the vanquished Cody had continued to implode. He'd overplayed his bravado at a new national magazine, refusing to revise an epic story; in an apparent revenge hire, Leviton took his rival's place on the masthead. Leviton's evil felt Shakespearean. He parted two Venetian slats to admire his fiancée in the driveway: she was leaning across the open hood of Leviton's hatchback, jimmying a new car battery into its brackets. Investing her devotion into the shared kitty of their future. All at once, her knees lurched. A wrench clanged to the pavement. She sent up a noise, something between a shriek and a roar.

Which of them thought to flood her eyes with the garden hose? Probably her, while Leviton phoned the urgent care on Western, the one with the 800 number on the awning. ("Battery acid!" he kept shouting, but with a slight accent, in lieu of knowing Spanish.) A week of oral steroids had saved her vision. But she'd spent herself broke on the doctor visit.

What had Dehlia wanted most? She'd been waiting, it seems to

Leviton, for him to be the guru—to make her detour as a lapsed daughter of privilege feel like a winning proposition, the same way Cody once had. And she'd tried to teach Leviton the script. She took housekeeper gigs to buy food. She repainted their extra room as his office—so that, with no loss of face, she could ask for a third more of the rent.

"That's not what we agreed upon," he said.

The thing was, he'd had every intention of going along with her request—so long as she knew he was not a man to be exploited. Not a man who needed to pay for love. Not an opportunist waiting for a damsel on the rebound.

"It would be honorable," she suggested. "It would be gentlemanly."

"What about your own income? I thought you were going to be typing a new resume."

"Excuse me? I was painting your room."

"I know that. And I'm incredibly touched and grateful. But, you know, you've also been sleeping in, every day, till, what, eleven? You wash your face till noon."

"You're timing me? In the bathroom?"

Leviton sighed.

"Is that who you think I am? Someone who'd marry you for the rent?"

"I am saying that agreements like this need to be discussed among grownups, not just performed to inflict guilt, if people are talking about marriage."

"You're being very shaming right now!"

"Yes, okay. We could both be more direct. You were trying to protect me, no doubt, from not getting something in return for shouldering more rent, but honestly—I'd have been fine with you just telling me you're short of funds."

"What I'm talking about is your tone."

Leviton breathed deeply. "We're both not at our best."

Her eyes shone from across their living room. Why did distance itself take a woman's side?

Even Bailey had warned him.

Still, the woman he'd chosen to phone from the stillness of that studio had been not Bailey but, rather, the lapsed B-movie actress who would become Philip's mother. Whatever else he could say about Nola, she'd never been shocked by tragedy, even as she was upended by everything else.

———————

At first, when he arrives at his Long Beach bungalow—collapse of shock absorbers, a shudder of pistons to dome-lit opacity—it's like he's cemented to the driver's seat. If he could sleep with hands on the wheel, he would. A pie of sand on the towel underneath.

But obeying who knows what deadline, he gathers valise, towels, Bailey's oversized shirts on hangers.

Staggering indoors with this armful, he'll still try, as always, to surprise himself with a panorama of the living room from toddler height. The treasure trail from Nintendo station to Dr. Dreadful's edible lab to the (refreshed on custody weekends) scatter of picture books on the coffee table. All laid out by Leviton to seem like discoveries. What is the opposite of an obstacle course?

The book's cover atop his sofa features Disney's bipeds Goofy and son Maxie, inseparable, side-hugging at the beach—from this image, Leviton had crayoned a portrait to hang on Philip's wall.

It is a wonderment to pee; then Leviton strips off jeans and trunks, and under the hot shower he tries to inhabit his bachelorhood in its saddest, most unredacted form—only he keeps failing at this, because loneliness to Leviton can't ever stop feeling like a prelude to some surprise that would make more sense. Also, it feels good to let himself be an ass about the subject of Bailey. Would it have killed her, for example, to lose weight? With the lather in his hair, he lets himself say it.

Which is when he feels, brushing against him, a consideration that strikes him as brilliant and apocalyptic both at once.

Bailey, of all people, might welcome his honesty.

Nothing is alien to art. No limits, no silent alarms. It's all human territory as far as the eye can see.

Hadn't she said, offering him the shirts, "I'm doing something new"?

As when he writes for an audience of one—an audience of Bailey—Leviton entertains, and then stares down into, the tunnel of possibility which says that whatever makes a thought delirious to the world's eyes is the thing that makes it noble and inspired.

He mauls himself dry.

But the bedroom phone feels like lead in his hand.

Because, fearless sounding board that she is, she is also a person. She can be hurt.

But with whom else could he confer, uncensored? Any presence he can imagine defers to hers.

"You're awake!" he says when she picks up.

"So are you!"

"True. Although, I could be faking." Since he doesn't land the tone quite right, he ends up laughing before she does.

"Are you okay?" she asks.

The very wrongness reminds him to press on. "I guess I'm double-checking. About the shirts."

"Enough, already, with the shirts!"

"Sorry. I do feel guilty taking them."

"Honest. Give them away if they don't work for you. I got tired of the—what do they call it: the dad look. The boyfriend shirt."

Try another door. "I get that. What's coming down the pike then?"

"My pike? The world's pike?" A pause. Bailey isn't quick to self-analysis. "Maybe I just want people to see a person instead of a caricature? I'm wanting to be lighter. I want to give books away too. I don't know if I'm making sense."

Was this an opening? "Lighter, like—do you think you should lose pounds?" With any luck, he sounds safely curious. Perhaps even opposed.

"I used to think about it. Only now—I'm not following."

He'd felt a current before, a wave of spirit, but it's gone. This has to come from him alone.

"Do you think about it still?" He flops backward onto his bed with the phone. "I guess I'm just picturing it. I guess I'm kind of liking it."

Her silence is so prolonged he is forced to go all in.

"Earlier, you were frustrated how I fell for everyone else—"

"After everything," she begins.

The train has left the station, his ticket is punched, and she is saying, "I just can't believe you did that."

"I felt I owed it to us." He has failed to keep things present tense.

"And, no. I'm never going to lose weight."

"This isn't all my fault. You basically asked me."

"And now you told me."

Leviton takes this in, ashamed—and then furious, betrayed—not by her being hurt, per se, but by his idea of what the great Bailey would have *done* with being hurt. They'd have talked and talked in her apartment, played records, and imagined themselves characters in a life. And she'd have lassoed their unclassifiable friendship mid-air, in silver stars. A constellation, a modern myth.

Nor can he describe why he feels duped by fate into bringing this new reality about.

"I'm aware!" he says. "I hear you saying I shouldn't have done it."

––––––––––

The drift between them will be gradual.

No longer her enthraller, Richard Leviton will become the beneficiary of Bailey's unsentimental judgment. Some of his stories are greeted with murderous indifference; others, lifesaving praise. He's almost phobic to ask what she thinks, until he knows he has to, until he's already internalized the worst possible truth in advance. Sometimes an artist can't afford the muse.

He submits long ideas to Kevin Claire in writing. One yes. One "Thanks all the same, but we'll pass."

In June, after handing in one of his hazier essays (something about songs with "secret Southern California geographies"), he barely averts a fact-checking fiasco: His reference to a pilfered photo, now four bolts in the wall, at the McDonald's Museum in Downey, identifies President Bill Clinton, but where is Leviton's source? Has he merely assumed? He spends a panicked weekend voicemailing the young corporate publicist; miraculously, having dropped in to retrieve a pair of running shoes on a Sunday, she tracks down an answer: *That would be JFK. Yes, Clinton also knows his way around a hamburger. Is there anything else?*

Thus Leviton escapes the spectacle of the fact desk reaching Bailey with a correction before he does, but her tone? Suffice to say, she is not the expense-fudging contemporary he'd met for lunch in 1983, when she joked, "Make sure we spend a minute discussing your piece." All the outlandish creative liberty she'd extended him over the years had been balanced against the (obvious, obvious) understanding that, even for visionary feature writers like Leviton, facts were sacred. Journalism 101.

This is not to say that Leviton's shame doesn't also bring a measure of spooky relief. He's a deposed president, a fallen star, a vanquished race. He contemplates growing a beard. On his fortieth birthday, he decides he'll swim in the ocean near his Long Beach home alone. The murky table of the South Bay, blocked by the Palos Verdes peninsula, both shuns and shelters him. Cold water heavy in his trunks, he trudges to waist depth—you're never more aware than when wading into water of whatever kind of misassembled creature you must look like from behind—maybe never more yourself. As long as he's lived he's been either ashamed of this view of himself or trying to compensate. A small plane, whose ad banner he can't read, tows its shadow across the surface of the sea, and he remembers the interesting disturbance he felt that day in Venice: a splice, a strobe, a magician's black cloth, as he dives into the cold. Is that what it is to be free in this world? The day of his birth and no one's eyes over his shoulder, no one watching him at all.

There You Stood on
Your Feather: 2010

THE FIRST TIME PHILIP said "Your generation had it all, didn't you," there was sad wonder in his voice, none of the sniping tone that seeped out later. It was like he'd been granted someone else's luck for just a minute and caught a glimpse of a world he always figured existed but had been born too late to see. And he seemed unsure whether to feel vindicated or persecuted about that.

We'd been hiking on his visitation night to get orange sodas at Ralphs and to reenact the permanence of him and me. And to be away from my fights with Wanda, my evangelical second wife, about mortgage renegotiation and whether I was getting enough proofreading jobs to compensate for the latest faculty furloughs. I wanted him to feel released in the night air from his complaints about teachers mocking him or singling him out—not a constant theme yet, but familiar enough that his four-year-old half-sister, Zooey, had asked at dinner, "How was school today, Philip, was it horrible?"

That April in our neighborhood in Long Beach, 2010, was no longer so chilly that all the delinquent Christmas lights blurred in our eyes like watercolors, but there were breezes, and our hands were in our pockets as we strolled and talked. We'd reached the crumpled guardrail that divided the stucco homes from the Unocal station at Cherry and Carson when I realized that if we stood exactly where we were, if we focused our eyes on the 30-foot gunite-and-steel donut atop the corner donut stand, we were going to experience a celestial event. The full moon, rising, was about to be captured within the hole of the Angel City donut.

Who knew whether that cosmic positioning had ever occurred? Unless maybe it happened every time the moon was full, depending on where you stood, and no one else but the two of us could be so dumb. But that sort of honesty was exactly what I loved best about being with my oldest son whenever we were finally away from everyone else.

So he waited for me to focus my flip phone camera, while I tried to think of Facebook captions in advance—all of which nearly worked, although never quite: *A-OK from Angel Food Donut! Keep your eye on the donut hole!* The photo was a delicate operation, too. You had to hold your angle steady for the precise instant when the rim of the moon adhered to the upper rim of the donut hole without yet detaching from the base—I was sure there'd be gaps here and there in the border where the fabric of sky would show through.

Somehow, though, for just a heartbeat—click!—there were none.

I released my breath, pocketed the phone, and started whooping and laughing, awkwardly high-fiving Philip.

No one who saw us, of course, would have any idea what our euphoria was about. Everyplace but Ralphs had closed, and cars and trucks merely zoomed by, although in a perfect world they'd have been honking, flashing their lights or cheering us on. I started asking Philip all the suddenly relevant questions about lunar orbit and lunar phases that he probably should have been asking me, and he could only protest "I don't know!" each time. But the fact was, looking back, he wasn't enjoying the helplessness like I was.

"You okay?" I shook him lightly.

There was a fragile look about his eyes. "You already know. Don't you?"

"Already know what? I'm lost."

"We're allowed to talk?"

I looked around as if to say: who's here to stop us?

"I'm worrying about culture."

"You're worrying about culture."

He nodded.

"Is there a way to narrow it down?" I was trying to sound teasing. It was such a slight, eerie discontinuity that first time—like the ground shifting, or the sway of a rope bridge.

When he didn't smile, I just stood still and breathed deep through my nose—my habit when I'm trying hard not to express frustration and thereby have done so. Then the crossing light turned green.

I'd passed through my own adolescence knowing that I possessed a certain mysterious kill switch to major fear—a secret trick that had only ever revealed itself when I was hopelessly alone. It was like suddenly being made wise to how futile helplessness was without ever daring to go all the way into it, the way many people did. Only as a father did it hit me that there might be people, like Philip, who lacked this instinct (had it been shaken into me? no, because I'd tried shaking it into Philip and never could). And I sometimes wondered if maybe that was The Plan—if maybe I'd been picked to be a sensitive child's guide because I knew both conditions, the fear and the disappearing-fear trick. I also wondered if God was somehow rooting for us down here, this minute, to be the team he'd picked us to be. Me holding the lifeline that God had thrown me in my youth, and Philip holding on to me.

So I decided the thing to do inside Ralphs was riff with Philip a little about how far-reaching and nebulous "culture" was. How it was maybe a totally reasonable thing for a precocious kid to worry about. Especially if he thought he needed all this figured out to be initiated into adulthood. We talked about game shows and pop music that we both liked or both didn't, and whatever dumbed-down version of French critical theory we could get away with misunderstanding, and I think he genuinely began to feel better as long as I was talking. The fluorescent lights inside Ralphs made the store feel like a safe island—a night kitchen.

"Can I get this book for us?" I had brought our sodas to the register, where a rack of paperbacks titled "Prayers for Emergencies" filled me with wholesome longing.

I'm Angry with God, one prayer was titled.

I'm Brokenhearted.

I Feel Unsafe at School.

Philip shrugged—not immediately rejecting—then added, "It's probably bullshit."

"'Bullshit?' I don't get you anymore. How come I can appreciate this but you don't? The same things used to move us. The same songs on the radio."

"Yeah, well, that's the point, isn't it?"

"What is?"

"Your generation had it all. You had the bands, you had everything. You lived the life."

"That's right," I declared. I was letting myself gloat, but I was also conceding to his sadness. "My generation had life easier, in plenty of ways."

The walk home took us between two cemeteries, and several of the streets curved for no reason other than an attempt to create interest on a grid. Because of these curves, you could get turned around sometimes, but then you reached your own corner and were set right. There was our squat palm tree by the porch, and the trellis, which my wife and I had trimmed to the height of a porch rail.

"Let's not go in for a minute," I said.

I opened the trunk of my car to fling a Frisbee toward Philip, motioning him back a distance with my fingers.

Just then a car pulled up to the curb, and out came a couple.

"I'll give you a good price," the man called to me. He offered a business card as if he were kindly returning what I'd dropped.

"Price on what?"

"When you want to talk about the house, my number's on the back."

"That's okay. We're not selling."

"I'll get you a lot of your money back."

I bounced on my toes waiting for the toss from Philip—not

dismissing the stranger so much as flaunting, in a subtle way, this enviable suburban moment that I was sharing with a son, who was not yet too old to share it with me.

"We're not selling the house," I said. Unbelievably, it hadn't hit me how inappropriate this all was, approaching me in front of my family.

"It's okay, Ed," the woman said.

The man said, "If your goddamn address shouldn't be in the foreclosure listings, maybe get it removed."

I nearly apologized, his irritation caught me so off guard. But the woman pulled him by the arm, and while turning to leave they nearly bumped Philip off the curb, an indignity I felt in my body before I could even have named what it was.

There were the rapids and then the falls, and with each branch and twig that we clung to and tore along the way, it seemed more clear he'd be heading with me to Silver Lake, the shimmering pool. Although for sure we might have chosen better circumstances.

How it happened was after the bank kept asking Wanda for the same paperwork, never acknowledging receipt. And after the June Bugs picnic when Philip wandered off and voice-mailed me from the outskirts. "I think there's something wrong with me, Dad, I think I need to *be home*."

For years, I saved that recording.

I won't describe it in a sentence, will I. Something about the happy age he used to be and what fraction of that voice could still be heard in this one, trying to stay with us.

"Have you had thoughts of harming yourself?" the Kaiser doctor asked when his mother, Nola, brought him in. "Have you thought about a method?"

Philip answered, being cooperative, "I thought I could put my head in a bag."

The other thing I'll never describe is Nola phoning from the examining room, begging me to stop the process, knowing I couldn't.

111

As if her voice had found the exact inevitable sound she once married me hoping never to make.

After he got out of the two-week hold, I drove with Philip cross country and back, fantasizing that doing something crazy would change our luck. Because or in spite of the Prozac he'd been prescribed, he experienced a few strange body phobias—did this dry skin mean his dick was falling off? But after phoning Nola for reassurance, he fell right to sleep—then we got traction. We drove 900 miles a day until he'd learned to drive a stick. From a tent site in Elk City, I felt so free that I even phoned Wanda, believing that her voice held a gust of admiration for the two adventurers.

If I could speak to the self I was then, I'd say: Don't forget that this was real, and it was yours. Because in a month, Gemshore Bank will claim they never got the mortgage forms you mailed each week.

And the lawyers you consult will sigh, because there are millions out of luck in 2010. Take the relocation cash, they will say, while you can.

It will also be Wanda's chance for daylight, to rent a small apartment across from the park in our Long Beach neighborhood.

And it will be Philip's window to live with me in the city, where on the basis of my past, and some old magazines, and a lot of the music he has loved, he's always been given to hope he might belong.

That, along with a hazy idea of wanting to live and grow old among dreams and dreamers—that feeling, unique to Los Angeles, of a syllogism always on the verge of completion. The way envy would feel, if envy were more like a promise, or a kind of maddening hope.

Before even unpacking, we took off like freed men for the newly christened Silver Lake Meadow beside the famous reservoir. The sod was barely planted, but you could already see parasols and a multitude of redheads keeping themselves pale in the December sun. Men over fifty in bright-colored Keds kept jogging past, and I remember wanting them to admire our solidity, acquired in a blue-collar town, while also accepting us as their own.

We were renting spare rooms from Casey, a woman I had dated in my twenties (because how else do I know anyone). When we returned from the park, Philip and I wedged our jackets and boots into an entry closet, while Casey waved through the open front door across the street toward a neighbor woman with flowing gray curls—an adjunct art instructor, Casey said, who also occasionally took boarders.

"But she doesn't want any right now," Casey said, "and she's going away for winter break in Europe."

"To Europe? On an adjunct salary?"

"Well, she also does other things, too. Something to do with agit-prop that uses textiles and performance."

"Textiles, agitprop, performance? Gets you a second home in Europe?"

But our landlady didn't fight or frown. When Casey dealt with agitated people, she only smiled a different sort of sadly courageous smile. It was a thing about her that I'd been attracted to thirty years before.

When driving back to Long Beach to get some more of Philip's things, or to drop by my Cal State office, I would feel myself crossing, then dropping into, the event horizon of the ten years I'd spent married to Wanda. In line at Starbucks, I spotted a guy we'd known in AA as Minnesota Doug. Outside AA meetings, such a nickname would derive from an interesting story, but no. Though barely half my age, he always dressed like a silver sneakers guy in a pharmaceutical ad (track suit, hair freshly combed), and he never shared his own deep feelings, just claimed to admire you for sharing yours. He had a way of sidling up like a protégé. "I heard about you and Wanda," he said. "That's got to be hard."

"It is," I said. "I mean, I'm hanging in there, but it's hard."

We had an awkward pause—so I added a couple of sad details about the timing, and how worried I was for the children—modeling, I guess, this intimacy he admired that I wasn't sure I felt. Doug's hand went to my shoulder. "Man. I just feel for you both. I really do."

Then I went by Wanda's to get my unforwarded mail while she was out. There were credit card bills, a DMV renewal form, and a new issue of *The Sun*, whose "Readers Write" section that month was all about divorce. One writer lamented that in a custody hearing she'd had to remind herself not to straighten her ex-husband's tie. *Look,* I said to myself—but I meant it for Wanda—*there are wives who love their husbands like that!*

I went down the entry stairs to sit in my car and started filling a notebook with dark, prophetic letters to *The Sun*.

I warned righteously about our nation's failure to adapt to an age in which all the marriages were being ended by well-preserved women. An age in which my wife could snap dance-floor selfies with her niece on social media. But any father who dreamed of celebrating bachelorhood with his son was an inherently disgusting and unlovable creature.

I wrote until it was necessary to turn on the dome light, then tore up the pages and drove to Nola's, where Philip had gone for dinner.

But first I rolled down the window and let myself shriek into the night like a dog with a broken back—repeating *no one cares, no one cares,* on the 405 South, and finding some odd kind of togetherness in self-pity.

———————

His curls were frizzing out in a humiliating way that I had to resist thinking only Philip's could, but as victimized as this made him feel, he preferred to feel victimized than to ever spend five seconds using hair products. Because, and this was very Philip, either it was pointless to try or unjust for him to have to.

Because in his eleventh-grade bloom, he had needed only to roll from bed and throw on his jeans to spend lunch breaks leading around the dark-eyed Cleopatra who'd chosen him. The one whose father had the souped-up VW Bug, from the backseat of which she would emit to us the most hollow, hostage stare.

So Philip would rage about his hair to accuse his past of deserting

114

him, and I would follow him around barking life lessons like *Welcome to the world, Philip, where you have to do things to change things!*

Because who else would love him bravely enough to speak such truth? Least of all Nola, whose shame as a former B-movie starlet had driven her out of the world of physical appearances altogether. Whereas I could never. Not with his new life barely begun.

For example, he'd be living in his own back house. On our walk-through, Casey told us about the previous occupant—a teenaged kid with a hippie name who'd had two moms and worked in forestry. He'd led a band that had a new EP: maybe we'd heard of them? The toilet, which that teenager had added to bring the shed up to code, was unfortunately not connecting properly to the main line—maybe Philip would know how to fix it? Casey was a caricature of happy helplessness. A teenaged boy would figure all this out. In the interim, he'd better use the main house to pee.

The windows of his shed were bare so, from his laptop, I began bookmarking plaid curtains, hoping that they'd strike Philip as hippie or grunge, instead of K-mart Christmas Elves. Or would that be the coolest thing of all? "What do you think, Philip?"

But Philip had taken to his bunk.

"Do you think I'm doing this for me?" I said.

He got up and pointed out a set of brown ones.

"What about these?" I said instead, steering him toward green plaid.

He agreed, but listlessly, and I gave myself a time out. I walked from the shed across the grass, which felt like wet horsehair, and up the wooden staircase to the landing of my own room, overlooking his, giving him space, in a prisonyard way. In the winter sun, hotter as it radiated off the planks, I opened Leonard Cohen's *Book of Longing*, but the poems were so good I kept going inside, antsy about my own lapsed work. Would my next phase of life ever be monastic, would I ever whittle at ease like Leonard Cohen, would Philip bloom, would it ever happen here? The room I slept in wasn't even my room. On those days when Casey's ninth-grader, Jasper, returned from his dad's, I'd migrate to the living area, unhitching a new Ikea chair-bed, which looked like a torture device when upright. Specifically, I never slept in Casey's bed—although I'd wondered, at times, if that might be God's plan for skipping past grief. Remembering how, when we were young, Casey had a smile like a magician's volunteer, a smile waiting for the next wonderful thing to happen.

But now her smile wanted me to join in putting down her ex-husband, Dunton, whom Casey was suing for Parental Alienation of their son. And she had a strong case. "Fuck you, Casey," the son would say, calmly, if she invited him to join us for dinner.

She'd wait by his doorway, coaxing him in therapeutic tones, until he would fly down the steps of the side yard toward the bus stop down on Sunset, where, as Casey explained, he'd ride three bus connections to the father's apartment in Glendale.

Late at night, though, he'd be driven back—the ex-husband saluting me with a pariah's smirk from beneath the porch light as Jasper would encamp himself with headphones before the Xbox, staging all-night army raids while I huddled on the chair cot faking sleep.

When Daniel and Zooey arrived for their first overnight—he was eight and she'd just turned six—Daniel took the chair cot and Zooey curled beside me in Jasper's bed. I sang our traditional One-Line Beatles Song, zipping my lip because Her Majesty has nothing to say, but this worked like tickling a cancer patient: She was young enough to laugh without wanting to, and old enough that the indignity showed. I segued to prayer. I asked my daughter what to pray about. Ask God anything.

"For us all to be together in the old house," Zooey said.

What a girl.

I suggested that God would bring good out of whatever happened to us, although of course this came across as "I'm a phony when you need me most," and Zooey sat sobbing in total confusion, "No one told me there was any such thing as divorce!" It was a sentence I'd thought nearly verbatim when I was six.

But in the morning, Silver Lake managed to feel new again. Casey involved the kids with spades and hoes outside Philip's shed, planting God knew what. There was a boarder named Hao-Yu, a living pun, in English, but no one went there, whose sanity we shattered

116

people all secretly clung to—an exchange student studying makeup art—and that afternoon, he arrived back from the studio, extending Chinese confections for the children. He'd been assigned a movie to watch on Netflix, apologizing because he didn't want to commandeer the living room. The fact was, we'd have paid to watch a film with him. I think it was a cross-dressing comedy with Robin Williams or Dustin Hoffman, although Philip remembers something earlier, with Grace Kelly; either way, it was the best kind of Los Angeles night: Sitting before a TV in loyal decadence, and having it also be somebody's work, and seeing someone from another culture so grateful to inherit the sputtering torch of Hollywood glamour. As a gay man, he was possibly misunderstood in the place he'd come from (although not by his family, with whom he spoke late into the night), and I kept thinking, what a thing that is to be: a foreigner who makes all the Hollywood people feel at home.

In my one great Christmas Eve photo from Casey's, Daniel wears the Santa hat (if there's a hat, it ends up Daniel's), and Zooey, in pigtails and onesies, worshipfully readies a next decoration to hand him—so perfect a North Pole moment that I posted it online with the caption "Expecting to Fly."

Philip even let himself decorate a gingerbread house—though, on the other hand, mainly to eat it. He hid his desire behind a pessimism so practiced that his younger siblings took turns trying to do the work for him.

I was always misunderstanding what would excite him. It wasn't having his own shed; it was learning he was allowed to eat cookies in it. It was whatever I invented as a family tradition.

In January it was the taqueria across from City College, after I helped him enroll for the spring semester.

"Hey! Maybe Lucinda would like this place," he said when the chips arrived.

"I think she's experienced Mexican food," I said, irritably. Outside we could hear the chirp of the crosswalk signal to the Braille Institute, next door to the college, and it was continual. *Like a cuckoo clock*, I complained. *It's like it's always twelve o'clock.*

"It *is* twelve o'clock," Philip pointed out, which was actually pretty funny.

"How does it even help them cross?" I asked.

"Help who?"

"The deaf students. How does the chirping help them?" I was entirely sincere.

"What are you saying, Dad? Aren't they *blind*?"

"Philip, stop it! Braille is for—wait—"

Somehow, I'd slipped into a universe where deaf people studied Braille. And needed crossing signals to penetrate their deafness. I laughed—this felt like us again.

"I *thought* I was right," he said. "But you made me unsure."

"No, no, of *course* you're right, Philip." His willingness to believe any stupidity from me made me think no one should ever have such power. "And for sure let's have Lucinda over. Let's do it soon."

"Really? Her dad will insist on coming too."

"Well, that's no problem for me."

Five o'clock on Friday turned into six and then seven while Lucinda's father's Beetle tried to reach us through downtown traffic. Hao-Yu was away somewhere filming, and, it being my night to serve food, Casey was being conspicuously un-choosey. When the guests finally arrived, I moved the tray of supermarket tacos into a warm oven to reheat, while Lucinda's father, Sal, inspected the front room in a way that suggested he'd visited before, and that things were mostly as he remembered.

"Why not show Lucinda your back house?" I told Philip, and as they headed out, Sal let out a whistle that turned into a laugh. "Oh, boy. My wife would not be very good with that!"

"Sorry—should I bring them back?" I asked.

"No, man, for sure. I got no problem!"

But his face said otherwise—so after a minute we fathers followed out back. Even through the plaid curtains, you could predict

Lucinda's furtive expression. It was a certain Sphynx-like air that she always wore, but this time almost burning, as if we'd interrupted a fight. They were avoiding anyone's eyes, most of all each other's.

Dinner conversation seemed easier, at least for the kids, but Sal had to be invited to join in, again and again, as if he were only his daughter's chauffeur. At last, it occurred to me to get guitars. Lucinda knew every Beatles song ever recorded—she was either grateful for her parents' ban on the wider listening universe or she was destroying their pleasure by coopting it—so I asked Philip to lead us in something singable.

But he went esoteric. He'd play one complicated riff after another to songs that no one knew, stopping himself each time to confess he didn't know the words. I felt our guests begin to squirm, or maybe it was me.

I threw him one song title, and then another, but it was mostly my way of asking for a turn.

Finally he passed me the instrument.

So I chose a couple of woodsier Beatle tunes, which I said seemed made for the Silver Lake hills—"I've Just Seen a Face," for example, and "Heart of the Country." Casey hovered by the hallway, tapping time, and you could hear Philip's hesitant punk vibrato coming to life. I thought I was on a roll, so I launched into the old Dionne Warwick hit, "Do You Know the Way to San Jose," because I had the fingerings down to a silky autograph, and Philip probably knew I was showing off. But I believe my real purpose, which came clear to me only as I played, was for Philip to know that the song's message, about purity and young dreams, belonged, in some magic and timeless way, to him. You could feel it in the frail cheer of Burt Bacharach's melody, the story of a small-town heroine against the great big freeway.

That is where something went wrong. A minor chord opens itself into the most aching major seventh ("with a dream in your heart, you're never alone"), and I could feel something else take place, not for the first time: a phenomenon peculiar to Philip, where feelings, especially in music, can become Too Nearly True. He fled the room.

I hid my sense of alarm, held the final chord for a long reflective

119

time, then excused myself and found him by the door of his shed. He was neither quite inside nor out.

"Are you all right?"

"You know I'm not." Accusation pinched his brow.

If he was going to accuse me of upstaging him on guitar, I was going to defend myself. He could be so childish that way. We stared at each other while I waited for him to explain. But he wouldn't, at least not then.

Years later, Philip maintains I've misremembered the whole event. He'd gotten mad not in Silver Lake but the next Thanksgiving back in Long Beach; and I didn't sing Burt Bacharach but the Beatles' "Rocky Raccoon," specifically to taunt him, because the song's fictional hero loses his girl to a rival.

Your generation had it all. Didn't you. Are you one of them? Did you get to her too? This is Philip's inner voice, some days.

I believe my memory still has its truth. I think that there's a sense in which Dionne Warwick's voice and Burt Bacharach's composition in the 1960s anticipated, in their own way, the life of a special kid named Philip who had not yet lived. For who can say there aren't these kinds of timeless junctures to music and art. And it's with as much fatherly pride as grief that I tell you my son has struggled all his life to turn down the volume on those junctures: the human truths that issue from the walls every time their special melody or deep emotion is sung. Even when he was my gleeful son, he'd always seen and heard a bit too much.

But outside the shed all I did was touch his forehead and ask if he wanted to come in for dessert. "You're probably tired," I said. "Or dehydrated."

———

Later that night I lay a long time in the dark, trying to sleep, or trying to fool myself that I was trying to sleep. Then tiptoed to my valise and felt around.

Back when Wanda and I were planning weekly date nights—and

too often ended up at Souplantation, trailing sad corn muffin crumbs through melted ice cream—we decided to shoot a roll of erotic pictures at my office, and I kept just one: a souvenir.

It was my fantasy first, but Wanda confessed it also matched hers, so there was this great coming out, and only after the loss of our house could not be distinguished from every other thing we'd ruined did she inform me that I'd ruined this thing too. Sexy she had been all her life, but she'd never felt pretty. What a victory that photoshoot should have been! What a gift to us as a couple. She was raging to make her point, tears streaming.

When we packed up the house I'd gotten permission to keep the one. We were separating, I reminded her, not divorcing. Hadn't she always told me that, according to the Bible, we could not be "torn asunder"? I had a few tears of my own.

Thus it made Christian sense to Wanda that keeping a boudoir picture of my wife was a better outlet than other temptations I might turn to, and we bonded again in our lowness.

In the moonlight that penetrated the blinds, I stared at the photo. The dune of her hip, swiveling on a cold metal desk. One lovely, drawn nipple, stranded upward. I gazed until it felt dangerous to go farther, but turning away made me angry, which aroused me more.

I parted the blinds. Philip's light was still on in his shed.

Giving up, I put the photo back into the valise and stepped into jeans, imagining I'd drop by and we'd bond about sleeplessness with a cup of chamomile tea. In the kitchen, though, I changed my mind. I ate some yogurt by the light of the refrigerator and went back to bed in my clothes.

It turned out he'd been on the phone with Lucinda. She was starting to take charge, like an old-school girlfriend, of their relationship—making lists, for example, of things that she appreciated about Philip and assigning him to do one back. On our morning walk to the Tropical Café, he asked, "But what if I don't love her?"

"Then you're allowed to not say it."

"But what if you've said it and you're not sure it's true?"

"I'm curious how you're sure it isn't true. But you can still walk it back. Tell her you don't know if you're old enough to know what love means. Or be okay with the fact that you probably meant well saying it. You can always say later that you'd been confused. Or that you've grown confused. Look at my life."

"You're not allowed to lie about love." He was adamant.

"I'm not sure what you mean by 'allowed.'"

"What if I broke something?"

"Broke what?"

"What if it's—you know. Unpardonable."

The word that comes to mind for how he looked just then is hunted. He looked like a fugitive.

"What's going to happen to me?"

"You're a beautiful guy, Philip, do you realize that? To honor your words like that. That's all the retribution there is. The fact you take any mistake so hard. Nothing's going to happen."

"Maybe something did."

"Is this that thing again?" Once, before the hospitalization, he'd had the strangest outburst of remorse. He said he'd seen too many shows and movies in which men (he could barely breathe, pushing the words out) *exploited women*. Romantic comedies, sitcoms with Archie Bunker husbands. "Maybe you're seeing a kind of unvarnished reality," I had said. "We all *say* we disagree with exploitation, but you, Philip, you really grasp it."

"He's always cared about the underdog," Nola said. "That's who our son is."

True, but he also regretted being kind, or a "sap," and thought simplicity was a fraud, and all through childhood went back and forth between a sensitivity he hated and a coarseness that he couldn't remotely pull off. He failed to kiss the artsy girl in high school, his first crush, the one with the hip psychologist parents, because he didn't realize that she'd wanted him to. He refused every joint in the high school parking lot, but then felt he'd blown his chance at popularity by following a meaningless rule. Sometimes Lucinda goaded him to throw ice cubes at passing cars, told him that's what "hail" meant, the verb, probing his innocence and planting distrust. She had begun college too, at Long Beach City, majoring in modern dance.

"She's not so inexperienced," Nola told me. "I watched her. I watched her dance."

Meanwhile the artsy girl was also in his heart. Near Valentine's Day he begged a ride so he could bring her one of those feng shui cat figurines from Japan Town. She either collected them or Philip thought she would think him cool for knowing what they were. Without an address or a phone number (because they'd only communicated by IM, and he'd only been to her parents' place once, for a party), we had to drive every block of her Long Beach neighborhood. The differences from Silver Lake were stark. The wide empty streets. No parked cars in the daytime. In the passenger seat, Philip's monkey boots seemed stuck onto the wrong feet, his ankles splayed outward, like a marionette's.

Suddenly he recognized a crème-colored clapboard house.

"You're sure that's the one?" I said.

"I think so."

"I'll wait to make sure they let you in."

"No, I'm sure." But he looked miserable.

"You know you're going to be too hot in that sweater."

"I'm aware."

Why did I always do that to him? I knew he felt handsome in the sweater.

"Three hours," I reminded him. "Text me if I need to come sooner."

He climbed out, shut the passenger door and then reopened it, because he'd almost forgotten the gift bag.

"Take two," I said and winked. "Keep your phone on."

When he disappeared into their house I drove out of the artsy girl's tract, found a bagel shop, took a table with my laptop and a coffee and got no work done, although I didn't really mind. I felt I was savoring a very earned break. I rarely exhaled, it seemed to me, until Philip was gone. For a minute I was just any parent, with any teenage kid. I sipped the coffee. One day soon, he would launch.

But even that thought had some baggage. Fifth grade science camp was Philip's first time away, and back then I'd kept turning my nerves into excitement. He was going to learn how strong he was away from our watch. Nola and I in effect would be blindfolded, unable to mess this up.

He had looked so vulnerable leaving, but that was the beauty, you see, because all of us would be proven wrong by letting go.

The first bad sign was his duffle. Every change of clothing when he got back was still folded and clean. In five days he had not changed his clothes. What happened, I asked him. His eyes were moist but also pleasant, as if he had been waiting so long to cry he'd forgotten he could stop smiling.

Weeks later we heard about the bullies. There was no supervision in the cabins or the stalls. Other details were added over the years. Nola had wanted to sue.

Beside the laptop, my phone had lit up.

"Are you okay?" I said. "It's been barely an hour."

"Yeah. I'm on her porch. Can you come?"

"Did something go wrong?"

Climbing into the car, and keeping quiet at first, the way he looked was as if he wanted very much to share a sad story, but also wanted very badly for the story to be funny. I knew that he was going to tell me either way—there was a child's hope of rescue in his eyes, alongside a familiar fear of disapproval.

He explained that he'd opened the artsy girl's refrigerator and tried to take a bottle of beer, but that she told him not to, because her parents would notice it was gone.

"I probably blew it," he said, interrupting himself.

"But you put the beer back," I said.

No. The girl, too, insisted that was what Philip should do, put the beer back, but Philip, not wanting one more time to be the nice boy, laughed, "It's just a beer." She insisted he give it back, and he tried to underscore his superiority by untwisting the cap, only his fingers couldn't get it to turn. While he struggled on and on with the cap, it seems she may have karate-chopped him, taken the bottle out of his hand and told him to leave.

"You have to apologize, Philip! You know that, right?"

124

He did not know that.

At the same time, I could not rise above thinking that the spectacle was somehow funny, in the most cringing way, and it must have shown on me.

This was good enough for Philip. He said, "Hey, isn't that supposed to be what girls want?"

His voice sounded like he'd just gotten his own joke, but his eyes said don't ever not love me, you're my father. Tell me there's a way to fail so bad that people have to love you the way your parents always do.

———

I knew this doctor on the AA program, Steven Aldercott, who felt so bad for me. He was always on *LA Magazine's* list of Top Physicians in his field, which I think was gastro, and so concerned about random friends' illnesses outside his field that he spent his off hours reading up, in Philip's case gabbing about brain receptors and dopamine and navigating so many digital culs-de-sac of information in the medical databases you'd get concerned for him. I could picture his bored wife across the room as he talked on the phone with me into the night—once I even heard her complain.

If Steven Aldercott saw people a little too much as walking casebooks, it was with no loss of compassion, and yet he couldn't see how rare and pure his compassion was, only his limitation. Nor did the limitation quite discourage him, because he had no goal or hobby that excited him as much as one day understanding every last medical mystery he wanted to understand, while at the same time knowing no such victory was ever attainable.

I used to imagine him a sailor, locked in a whirlpool, and the futility of the whirlpool had become his sportsman's paradise. Until he felt everyone's pain and no pain at once. Or maybe I make this up to justify my use of his time. Obsessive thinkers make up AA—maybe that's all the key to Dr. Steve that anyone needs.

There would be times, after the failure of our Silver Lake experiment—back in Long Beach apparently for good—when I would argue very dramatically with God about whether there shouldn't be a Last Tear that a parent of a mentally ill child could cry, having learned that it changed nothing to cry. It wasn't that I was suffering any more than any of us eventually suffer when the natural things we dream for our children are no longer realistic, but that my ability to still feel devastated and still cry revealed that I was additionally a failure at being wise. My mother when dying of emphysema kept protesting "I don't know how to die" until she did; maybe I did not know how to grieve. I thought I'd grieved, but then Nola had picked up Philip for an afternoon, and I'd seen him march to her car, robotic from Abilify and Risperdal, at exactly the age that one has looked forward to attaining all through one's awkward childhood, and it hit me, as I doubt it hits most people until they're dying: I would never get through this. My spirit would never triumph. We would lose.

Panicking, but not knowing what there was left to panic about—except maybe just that—I waved goodbye to him through the front window and then retreated in terror to my room, recycling scriptures that used to "work," like the one where Jesus prays "Father, take away this cup," and the one that says God will "turn our weeping into dancing," taking colder and colder pleasure in them not working, because the truest thing about mental illness is its uniqueness, its inability to transcend itself through spiritual comforts, because in the end only bitterness will do as an object of comfort, because mental illness tears up every avenue to inner joy. But still you want there to be a God to love you for being bitter! And then I decided I'd go for a "coldblooded walk," a choice Philip would have approved. One of Philip's all-time favorite songs was called "Cold-Blooded Old Times," by Bill Callahan, with lines about a father storming to work, busting the gate—had he remembered my fights with Nola? In his cells, how could he not? For him to love a song like that. So I was guilty as well as bereft.

But before I could get out the front door I saw a manilla envelope inside the screen, with my name written on it by hand. The street was quiet, the world unchanged, even brutally so—birdsong and foliage, and beauty with all the justness simply sucked out of it.

I took the package inside to my bed. I was apparently still the kind of fool whose hopes rose opening a package. There was a notecard taped to the seal, and I opened it.

Richard, I don't know why you have been chosen to go through this, but I admire you. I can't imagine what it's like. —Steven

Inside was a hardcover book that he'd gone and bought, coauthored by a father and a son. The father was a British war journalist with all feeling bludgeoned from his gaze, an emptiness with which he almost shamed the camera, as if to say he'd seen humanity at its worst. The son was a schizophrenic patient, and there were photos of him fanned out, from different stages of his life. His child's expression I recognized at once. The glee that is a little too gleeful, the mischief that's a little too rascally. As an adolescent, bearded and bearlike, he looked simultaneously overeager and rebuffed. The only other face I'd ever studied that was so fatally unable to hide or to tell a lie was Philip's.

I had the same kind of intuition about faces on the subway in Boston, visiting Sylvie, seeing the way Boston mouths set in Boston faces were different, and were going to speak with Boston accents.

Outside my bedroom window I heard the scrape of a lawn chair on cement. The neighbor was setting up to barbecue. I pulled the curtains closed to think some more.

I remembered the nanny who could not resist him. All the fawning strangers and friends. Like the one from the Bronx with a showman's smile, saying again and again, *That kid's magic*! I remembered the way Philip the toddler used to drag a leg when walking, like a soft shoe. And the cleft in his slightly weak chin. "That's the thing," a cashier once told us, "That's what all the girls are going to swoon for." You don't notice how special things were till they no longer are.

You could always goad my son higher, or ground him deeper. You could get him to chug down the block yelling Choo! Choo!; after which you could relax him with a book. "*Me and my dad are lucky to have each other*," said Goofy's son Max, a sob of true feeling in my

127

chest, because I could feel my son feel it, and later the voice would be his, enlivening a point, a profundity I loved because I'd put it there, I'd lured my son to sink wide-eyed into the terrible and marvelous meanings of words.

He pieced together answers more sensible than the truth.

"What's this about?" he asked from his toddler seat when the car radio played The Four Tops' "Same Old Song."

"It seems the singer and his girlfriend used to dance all night long to a song. But after she left, the song didn't sound happy to him anymore."

Philip's expression fell. "Why did she leave?"

This was just months after his mother and I divorced.

"I don't know," I said.

He thought, then shrugged. "I guess she got tired of that song."

An old friend once pitched a plastic ball too hard in my backyard, and it knocked Philip down. "Oh, I know, that's the worst!" my friend said, trying to console. "I once took a pitch right on the Adam's Apple!"

Philip, a wondrous listener even through tears—he was four at that time—replied, "And that's why your neck is so fat?"

Then I took over the pitching. I was going to do what love does: lob a pitch that Philip could not fail to hit. A pitcher can feel it in his blood, the point where the sinking pitch meets the batter's swing on the curve of time. "You get one pitch," I told Philip. "And if you hit it over the fence, I'll buy you any video game you want. I bet you can't."

But I knew, that day, he would. I can still hear the sound of it.

Yet somehow, that kind of memory never grafted itself onto Philip's idea of himself. His excitement was for the video game, not the accomplishment. He never particularly expected to hit another homer. He was neither disappointed by failure, nor ever quite surprised by coincidence. You were never sure if this aspect of Philip was a sacred thing to admire, or a fatal flaw that needed to be addressed.

Once, he prayed to acquire a pet bird, and the next day our pool man friend brought him a cockatiel that was near-drowned in a customer's filter. Philip was overjoyed about the bird, but at the same time, he was terrified by the fact his prayer was answered. There's a way, I suppose, in which that makes sense.

Philip at seven was the child who felt most bitter about my new marriage and the end of our exclusivity. But whenever we'd hold a family meeting, he was always the most trusting and on board.

———————

Heartwell Park is a suspiciously underused but very pretty green-belt and lake across from Long Beach City College, a place where, now that classes had begun, Lucinda's parents could neither watch her nor forbid her to be. I knew that she and Philip had started to fool around, because he'd hinted, and I also knew the thing nowadays is to dignify a son's hesitations about sex if he feels hesitant, as my generation of boys never dreamed it was okay to be.

"Hey," I said, pulling the car up a little too close to the college. "I know the kids at church had the sex talk from their youth pastors. Did you sit through that too?"

Honestly, I'd have settled for talking to him in the language of Christianity, if I could find my way back into it.

"I already know you think I deserve to enjoy myself," Philip said. "Mom thinks I'm being pressured."

"I'm not sure it's that simple. Just don't make it an assignment when it's a gift. It's not like in porn. A first girlfriend is a magical thing. You get to discover yourselves. You get to be two people figuring out everything you never knew you were allowed to want."

I had the awful feeling we should be talking about anatomy. But I was making him uncomfortable.

"I'm sorry," I said.

He spotted her in the crowded student parking lot, but we were in a bus zone, with the poor luck of a bus bearing down just behind us, so I had to wave quickly and meekly goodbye to him at the curb—that was that.

Killing time at a bookstore in Lakewood, I got his text message a little while later, and drove back to the park to retrieve him. When he spotted me, he scurried criminally to the car. It is a wonder they

129

never got arrested in the bushes.

Back in Silver Lake, if this were any clue how things had gone, he sank contentedly into some homework reading, as if his room were a raft on a pool. I decided I'd write too, taking advantage of the study hall vibe. For the first time I felt vaguely normal about our life in Silver Lake. Around 8:30, we got the idea to take a break at a certain café we'd seen by the reservoir. I wanted to bask in the feeling of a neighborhood where people were working on things, and where the nights were as roomy as the days. On the general store bench outside the café, we'd seen women before, of all ages, in prairie dresses and boots. Guys in skinny suits and no socks. Strangely, the neon sign depicted a cocktail glass when the establishment itself was called "TEA." So Philip and I arrived pleasantly confused about whether this café was really a bar or a tea room or what.

There were some small Formica tables, with mismatched chairs, despite a menu sign featuring $27 appetizers, and I kept straining to see what sort of food the carefully scruffy patrons at other tables were having, but no luck.

"Can we sit anywhere?" I asked a server.

"Pardon?" He looked puzzled, as if we'd stumbled upon the first unanticipated snag in the restaurant's concept. "Where do you want to sit?"

"It's up to you, Philip."

The table that Philip picked had chairs whose seatbacks were aggressively straight, with crownlike spikes, and this ought to have made it impossible for someone's coat to slip off them, but that is what happened, every time I turned around—twice I was interrupted by the waiter handing me my jacket. On the second occasion, there was a rough tear at the armpit.

The drinks menu didn't clear up our confusion—it featured a long list of teas, but the sizes, in tiny italics, were *shot, snifter, and goblet*—and you had to specify whether hot or "upon rocks."

"*I have not the slightest idea what this place is even about,*" I whispered to Philip, who looked clueless, but trusting. I brought the waiter. "This thing that's labeled brandy—"

130

"Brandy-tea?" the waiter asked.

"Yes, forgive me, does that mean brandy *with* tea? Or a kind of brandy that *is* tea? I mean, tea that is—"

The waiter checked my menu. "Do you want me to ask? It's a local supplier."

"I'd better just have Perrier. Although, yeah, I'm curious."

"Actually, the manager's out," the waiter said.

"*I'd* like a Perrier," Philip said, not to be forgotten.

The Rolling Stones' "Wild Horses" came on the sound system, and the waiter spun his head toward the bar, or the kitchen, and said, "Very funny, but put on the Mavis. Or is it Ibis?"

"Either one," called a young patron, looking up from his book, and the channel switched to something indie-hipster that sounded as if it were being sung into a bottle.

At the table nearest us, a woman appeared to be editing video, so settled and stationed that I imagined we could just start talking, like people who'd missed the last bus of the night. But then I couldn't decide if she worked for the café or had simply made the establishment her office. A group of four other people, speaking French, lingered in the middle of the room, as if this were a foyer to someplace else.

"Well, we're on an adventure, are we not?" I said to Philip. "Every day a rite of passage." Had we moved to Silver Lake because I thought Philip would belong, or because Philip thought I would belong? I shifted in my chair and felt my foot drag something, a napkin I thought, but it was only my jacket, which had fallen again.

We finished our Perriers, as if that were our main mission, and I stood up and tipped too much money, figuring we'd either be more welcome the next time we came there or less.

———

Hillside balconies with ivory balusters in the late afternoon. "Your mom lived in one of those," I said as we huffed around the lake, "or similar."

I remembered her long-ago basement room. Stained carpets and a transom window through which you were somehow aware of the faeried canyons and the black lake outside. At a party, some of us had gotten Nola to recite her blue, self-mocking poems.

She had been starting to like me, and I had been teaching her to proofread. On more than one hot dry day, we'd climbed these staircase ruins. Possibly the same steps (I told myself) that Laurel and Hardy kept skidding down when trying to deliver a piano. We'd try to get her humongous lacy dog outside, or make a long trek to Millie's Coffee Shop because she'd left her car keys there—it was always something like that with Nola.

Sunset Boulevard was still just as vibey, although a lot more congested. I scheduled friends from the old *LA Weekly* days to meet me at Tropical on days when Philip had an afternoon class at City College. I'd wait for them with my Americano and then present myself for the first time in forever, back from Siberia. A couple of my old colleagues, Guy and Felicia, were editing a journal now, with Guy's inheritance, and they showed up looking like sultry crime investigators: her 1940s house dress, his note-taking into his phone whenever she told him to write a thing down.

Guy and I had the Twelve Steps in common, and he also once wrote for Bailey Kavanagh, whose high opinion of my writing Guy still liked to act hurt by. "Favorite living writer my ass."

"The thing is," I said to Felicia, "Bailey has a very special bias against writers who write well."

Felicia snorted, and I remembered her antipathy for Bailey.

"How is she?" Guy asked. "Have you seen her?"

"No, but I will," I said. "I've convinced Philip that Bailey was the first goddess of the LA punk scene."

"I thought you were more a sixties music guy."

"Just that one song you never got around to reading about." When Guy was hard up, I'd offered to pay him for feedback on a book proposal. "Let's not leave Felicia staring into outer space."

"Felicia lives in outer space," he said.

She had the most amazing Spanish face, triangular as a drama mask, if they made masks for inward cheer.

"I'll resend the proposal," I said.

"No. Hard copies only."

"But it's thirty pages."

"Policy is policy."

Felicia laughed and slapped his hand. "Ignore Guy," she told me.

"Anyway," he said, "I'm sorry things didn't go well with the evangelical wife."

"*Really* ignore Guy."

Actually, I didn't mind Guy's comedy, and when we talked about story ideas, I started to feel the buzz of relevance again. I was feeling hopeful I'd be writing again soon. As Felicia's laptop slapped shut, we all shook hands.

"You shouldn't have married that evangelical," he said one more time.

Another afternoon, it was Cassandra Hui. This was a woman I'd pursued during my San Francisco twenties, when she was serving drinks in a wife-beater shirt at Hamburger Mary's. She used to have the most diplomatic way of rejecting you, as if she were involved with someone else and wished she weren't, but she wasn't. Now she was a ceramicist who was married to a jolly-looking, whiskery mensch. When I told her about losing my house, she winced in hilarious pain. Then I told her about Philip's hospitalization, and she groaned empathetically.

"Seriously," I said, "fix me up with a friend of yours. There's got to be someone. We'll double date."

Only later did it hit me what I must sound like to a date: foreclosure, skidding through a separation, renting rooms in a house, troubled son.

Of course, I tried to write. But mostly I would sketch and leave the business of actual sentences for a more committed time. I would stretch my notepad time as if waiting for happy hour, when I would leave a hopeful placemarker. Five of those got you to a weekend.

The Super Bowl fell on Wanda's Sunday, but it worked for her to leave Daniel and Zooey with me while she went to an AA viewing party in Pasadena—although the very fact it worked so well for

Wanda began to plant a seed of annoyance in me. When she dropped the kids off at the door, I think everyone could see how I held back, how I looked like an inpatient in a home for abandoned husbands, and how it killed me to notice how much weight she'd lost, how she glowed in her new white cutoffs.

Casey met her with a friendly handshake—either elevating my stock in Wanda's eyes or destroying it—and Wanda looked much too pleased to meet her, too, before spinning toward her car.

"See you around game's end, then?" I asked.

"Not sure, Richard!" Wanda's eyes alluded to the kids and admonished me.

"Well, what time do you think? Eight o'clock?"

"Don't do this, please."

With the kids not even settled in, I excused myself from the living room. I placed a call to Steven Aldercott.

"I feel your pain, brother," he said. "And I'm glad I won't be running into her today."

"You mean you're not going to the party?"

"It's pretty far," he said. "And, I mean, Minnesota *Doug*." This was a joke I was supposed to have caught on to.

"I'm not—I don't get it."

"I thought—I thought that's what you were upset about."

"She's with Doug?"

Steve was silent an extra moment. "You were upset about something else. I've misunderstood you."

"I was upset about watching the kids so she can do whatever she wants, when she hasn't gotten back to me about starting couples therapy."

"I'm sorry if I made things confusing. I'm surprised to hear about therapy. Pleasantly surprised, I mean."

I had promised Zooey I'd get her a papaya smoothie at Tropical before the game. Down the steep hill, the kids and I tromped with my moldy leather football, making a game of catching the ball behind our backs with eyes closed.

"Why does it matter to have closed eyes if you can't see behind you in the first place?" said Philip.

My heart was pounding and it was difficult to breathe. A ball hit me in the upper back, then rolled lopsidedly downhill, but Daniel ran ahead and stopped it with his heel. He did this a few times, which quickly got old—you couldn't really play catch in the streets of Silver Lake.

The Super Bowl passed in a blur. Sometime around eleven, after failing to enjoy a board game that I felt Wanda would have invented a way to enjoy, I helped carry the kids to her van, searching Wanda's eyes for an affirmation of all the history there was to us carrying kids to that van. Then I waved my ironic sad-smiled goodbye. The divorce papers would arrive the following weekend, she said.

"Wanda, why the rush?"

"I made a promise to myself."

"And?" I said. "You're not the one who's breaking it."

"I gave myself a deadline! I need you to do this for me."

"Do this for you? Like a husbandly favor?"

But I'd married Wanda for that same singlemindedness. The more she reached for her Bible, for example, the more I felt it made us rebels, renegades, discarding the opinions of the world—now I was the one who wanted that, and she didn't.

There were trump cards for this emergency in her church, even though you had the feeling no one ever played them. (*If your brother sins against you, show him his fault. . . if he refuses to listen, bring it to the church.*) The next morning, I phoned the young pastor, Brent, his voice a soul handshake until I made my request.

On Friday, there I was pulling in to a half circle driveway with camper shells and sports cars a half block from the Lakewood golf course. Six or seven church elders sat around a glass coffee table in the study. Dogs and home-schooled teenagers, wrapped in beach towels, rushed in unison to the doorbell to be disappointed. These were aging Jesus freaks, most of them, people baptized in waterfalls in Hawaii.

"John," I nodded, and shook his pool man hand solemnly. To the slender piano teacher beside him, I said, "Hello, Claire."

"How is Philip?" asked John's wife, Barbara.

135

"So much better," I said. "I don't want to brag, but he's really turn-ing a corner. He's riding buses, he's cooking meals."

"We're so relieved to hear," she said. "I caught sight of him one time, with his mother at the beach, and—" She looked down. "I remember wishing so strongly he could establish some distance from her."

Suddenly, appallingly, I seemed to have the floor. They already knew why I was there, and I framed things in their language. I talked about how impressed I'd been that the New Testament's first mira-cle, as they'd always taught me, was at a wedding. How the devil's greatest triumph was to undermine a marriage. "I'm only telling you what you all taught me. That's why this is so personal. Those days we rode together on your pool route, John. You were like a father to me."

Brent turned toward his wife, Rachel. "Didn't you talk to Wanda just today?"

"Richard," said Rachel, "we've tried. She's not open to discussing things at all."

"Of course, that's what she *would* say," I said. "That's who she is."

"Man," Brent said, "her tone. It's just done. Done with this."

On the contrary, I said—bear with me—just a few months before, when I'd followed the daily exercises in a certain workbook from the marriage ministry, with the courting and the bringing of gifts, things had been simply wonderful—Wanda even said so. Until she found I'd used a workbook. "What that says to me is we were incredibly close to a breakthrough. She won't say it because she's proud, and it scares her to think of not being proud, and her language isn't words. Did you hear about the sofa? The incident with the sofa?"

They all shook their heads blankly.

"In the middle of all our turmoil, Wanda had been sleeping on the living room couch. It was the only thing that supported her back. The place where the cushions met gave her just the right support in just the right place. And we couldn't afford a new bed. But after weeks and weeks of sleeping apart, I started to suspect that the bed was an excuse. So she said, *look: We'll move the couch into the bedroom. We'll place it alongside the bed, make one giant bed, and we'll be sleeping together again.* So we were going to, but the sofa wouldn't make the turns in the hallway. It was that deep, burgundy couch. Her prized possession from the death money her first husband left her.

"Anyway, you know Wanda—when she starts a job, she finishes it. She got out the chain saw. 'What are you doing?' I said.

"'I'm proving that I care,' she said.

"'No,' I said, 'we'll figure something else out, your point is proven.'

"But she went ahead. It was like a sacrament. She chain-sawed right through the fabric to the frame to remove the back of the sofa from the front. This incredibly well-made sofa. It took fifteen minutes to cut through all the construction. When it fell backward from the seat, it was like we'd exorcised a demon. Like we'd rescued a baby from a crate. It was like anything was possible.

"We hoisted the seatbed upright and slid and pushed and pivoted it down the hall. Pretty audacious and pleased with ourselves, pleased with the great story this was turning into. We were going to be bigger than our fate. But this time, unbelievably—it was the height of the door frame that stopped us. There was no way to tilt the sofa back and limbo it in, because right there, the hallway doglegs. The wall was too close. It was like, in our vision, we'd been to the promised land, but then we'd gotten cocky, and couldn't enter it.

"Maybe if we were somebody else, or if we had money, this might have been funny, or we could have celebrated the fact that we cared this much, but now it was all too charged with the way she felt cursed by her life. She said, 'We're not done, we're going to feed it through the bedroom window.' I had a premonition that we were doomed, but we kept moving. The tape measure said the sofa was an inch too wide for the window even with the scrolled arms removed, but our logic was: the frame could bow an inch. So that's how we finally failed. I was in the side yard and Wanda was inside, both of us huffing and sweating more than really exerting any traction on the sofa. We couldn't afford another bed, and we couldn't afford another sofa. God didn't help us, and you fuckers didn't help us, and you still don't. Half of you were at our wedding, when Brent said to everyone in attendance, 'Do you promise to do everything in your power to uphold this couple in their marriage?'"

"I just want you to know that I feel you," said Brent, much too soon, but that was my fool's victory.

And the rest of them stayed silent, not so much embarrassed, I think, as paying respect to how painful all the mountains are that faith can't move.

"Fuck you all," I added, to watch them prove their tolerance by staying calm, which they did.

Then I left, wonderfully alone, and phoned Wanda. Always we'd been bigger than the church. We'd blown off their advice when we rushed into marriage. "I want to talk about these papers. I'll control myself," I said. I would bring lunch, someplace public. That playground by her place with the zebra bench that Zooey loves.

"How nice," she said, with her blind, almost deranged receptivity. Chastely flattered at the fact of being wooed. Or perhaps hers was the voice of a wife who sees the meadow that begins the new, separate, friendly us.

I drove to her neighborhood through Paramount, where pickup trucks began to outnumber cars and the surroundings were as cheap as a KOA, but also happier, coarse manners make good neighbors, past firework stands and sandwich boards advertising the price of cigarettes. All through our Harbor Area marriage I had wanted to find sanctuary in the absence of snobbery. Not that we weren't ambitious in our own way. Wanda required the children to read two hours and write an essay each morning in the summer. She required them to work as counselors at Vacation Bible School and to visit museums and library events in the late afternoons. She ordered snow days in the middle of the school week if the tips of the San Gabriels turned white. Our parties featured laser tag, and glow sticks after dark. I could be too smart in my wife's eyes, but not too simple. This kind of wife, who wants a husband to be simple and brave and strong, seemed to be all I'd really wanted in the years that I chased complicated women. And when we married I had wanted her approval extra badly because it is never your simplicity that shames you in the very end.

Three blocks from San Antonio Park was the Panda Garden restaurant, where Wanda loved the egg flower soup. I purchased the large bowl in two Styrofoam cartons, hoisted in a plastic bag like a cradle from a stork. I drove to the north side of the park and there she was, on the zebra bench twenty yards from the swings. Annoyingly, she played with her phone. To replace the annoyance, I reminded myself that my wife and I had always struggled to understand each other's personalities, and that working on this had been a glue that sometimes bonded us. Breaking up could feel like something to begin from. Maybe now I was going to say goodbye to the idealistic fantasy version of our marriage the way Wanda already had.

"Soup," I announced, sorting the contents of the bag onto the bench. In my seriousness I felt handsome.

As if a nervous joke, she moaned the words *egg flower* a couple of times, in gluttonous hypnosis. "Do I owe you money?" she asked.

"Oh, come on."

A silence. "Well, thank you. How are you guys settling in up there?"

"Oh, you know," I said. "Philip misses you, actually. I'm not laying guilt. Just letting you know that he always appreciated the way you used to talk with him."

"The way I gave too much advice, you mean."

"He appreciated that too."

"He didn't seem to." She slurped the soup.

"I think your advice often soothed him. Even if he never felt capable of using it."

"Like I always told you: Me as a teenager? Holy crap, I needed structure. But my father, God bless him, was being a good liberal. I'm sorry, but he had no idea. Like I always say."

She was swinging one flip flop repeatedly out front from her toe until it slipped into the sand, and then she had to set the soup down on the bench to get the shoe.

I was struggling with Wanda's obnoxious favorite mannerism, the use of *sorry* to mean its opposite. It always embarrassed me, and I wanted to protect her from it.

"Well, Philip's catching up," I said. "He's learning to be independent and figure things out. Casey's son, for example, is way worse off than him. Divorce is a catastrophe for any kid." I wondered if I'd gone too far. "Casey's not a girlfriend, by the way." It seemed a good time to get this across. "We've never so much as hugged."

"Well, that's not my business."

"It is, though." I was sobered by the truth of this. But Wanda looked away. "I'm not here to fight," I said.

"I know. I appreciate that."

"I'm anxious to go to therapy with you. But today I'm just willing to listen."

"Richard. I don't have anything to tell you."

"You could tell me one thing you needed the most. Anything not to do this to our kids."

"Watch it, Richard. I'm doing this *for* them."

I held my tongue. "I've been thinking counseling might be useful whether we stay together or not. Didn't you say we were separating to get some objectivity?"

"We can get counseling," she said. "But not together."

"You're dating Minnesota Doug," I said. Taking advantage of the neutrality we seemed to have found.

But she nodded hilariously, as if I should share in her amazement.

"Wow," I said. "It's so not what you're about."

She wiped her mouth with a paper napkin.

"We're still married, Wanda."

"Actually, we became adulterers when we remarried. If you want to be biblical about it."

"Are there others? Besides Minnesota Doug? Teddy Bear Bill? Maybe the Boston Strangler?"

"Sex partners, you mean?"

"Who brought up sex?"

"I went out with a few guys from the Saturday meeting. But they started calling during crunch time, with the kids trying to do homework, and that wasn't going to fly. Sorry, but hello?"

I was moving around cleaning up our trash, wondering how anyone but me could stand her, and wanting her so.

"I guess you've prayed about it all."

"After where prayer got us before?"

"Come on," I said.

"You come on." Now she was mad. "We caved and had sex and then got married to keep having sex. And our marriage was hell and I'm glad as hell that I'm never going to do that again. That wasn't God."

"It was," I said. "Look at these kids."

But my conviction could not equal hers. Not in religion or against religion. Not in marriage or against marriage.

"That's what's going down in your church," I would be sure to fink to Pastor Brent. "That's who's teaching in your Sunday School."

Instead, when I got back to Silver Lake, it felt possible I had achieved some kind of release. I found Philip in his shed, where he asked for my help editing a Humanities paper. Here I belonged. He'd reviewed an exhibit at the Grammy Museum, with photographs of rockers like Madonna, Debra Harry, and Joan Jett. It was the kind of school experience he always should have had. He was quoting bell hooks on Madonna—it was a solid first draft.

How I'd missed him. He'd been braving so much on his own. He'd boarded buses in the wrong direction, not grasping that the side of the street on which you stood determined which way the bus would be traveling.

"Commas inside quotes," I said. "Always, in American English. Look, Philip," I said, "do you want to go to Griffith Park before it's dark? That's how I always used to end a writing day when I was younger."

At one of those lawn-sized pastures near the park entrance, we broke out the Frisbee. There were thicketed hillside trails to one side and the main road on the other. "One," I called, as Philip cradled my first toss to his middle. The ritual was you had to complete ten throws without a drop, only now I was getting so old I could barely trot to the disc each time it fell. Yet here he was, willing to play with his dad, and why should I assume my sadness about losing a house and a marriage was any worse than his?

That night we did another LA thing—we stopped by a photographer friend's exhibit south of Sunset. The building resembled a Boy Scout den or a union hall, its rutted parking lot surrounded by fig trees. The four walls of a single rectangular room were lined

141

with matted frame photos, all depicting backyards and decks and barebacked canyons, and the viewing was so jammed that we soon found ourselves in a clockwise herd. Philip looked handsome and lean, wearing a tan zip-up jacket from the Army surplus, but even so, I knew his social anxiety could be devastating. "You sure you're up for this?" I said.

In a far corner my old friend waved, through a swarm of well-wishers.

"You might remember him," I told Philip. "He came over for ribs once, in Long Beach."

"Oh, that's right. Look at this."

It was a photo of a sparse pool deck, which Philip pronounced "nihilistic."

"This is your son?"

The voice belonged to an older woman, gray-ringleted and glowing without makeup, and of a taller race. In Silver Lake the manic pixies don't grow old but tall.

"Yes! And he's a student at LACC," I babbled.

"Oh! Good for him! Studying art, then?"

I could see Philip straining to answer, but this once, his strain had precisely the charm that it deserved. "Right now I'm taking some of everything," he said.

"Samantha?" The woman's friend cut in. "We're getting more champagne. Do you want something?"

"Just a bottle of water," Samantha said. "Aubrey, this is—"

"Tell them your name, Philip," I said, thinking, shit, I've undermined his grownup mojo.

"Well, now he doesn't have to," said Samantha.

Philip, by skill or luck, ad-libbed, "This is my father, whom I call Dad."

A path to my friend opened then, but a group of other guests got there first, which was fine, because for a moment I could behold Philip from a distance, conversing with these three gray-headed hippies, their bangles and gowns moving in a breeze from the open door. For some reason, the one named Samantha had begun singing a verse of something, in a trial balloon way, inquiring if Philip knew it, and Aubrey had begun to harmonize—it was something canticle-like, Renaissance music, graceful as a stem.

Might they have been a professional duet? I tried and tried to think what I'd label these singing strangers if I were writing a script for a movie—nymphs? Sirens?—but those had nearly opposite meanings. In any case I'd found my way to Dominique now. "We have to leave in a minute, but I'm so glad we came by," I said. When we left, I had never felt more excited for Philip or more hopeful.

———

The car ride to Bailey Kavanagh's, on the evening Philip and I visited, circled downtown from the north and then out west past half the neighborhoods I'd ever lived in.

Here were the Police Academy and the sanitarium, where phalanxes of recruits used to run up the Echo Park hills. I always heard them chanting as they passed.

Here was a bachelor apartment I'd nearly rented, in the eighties, way back when Dehlia threw me out, that dropped three steps down from every alcove to the next—I guess that's how they dealt with the hillside slope—and a ceiling as low as the inside of a van. To make the deposit, I'd had to spend an hour inside a phone booth on Fletcher Drive, begging the editor of *Premiere* for an overdue check.

Then west past the old On Club, a reggae place, where I hadn't loved the music quite as much as the dance, like marionettes, like lifting your feet from tar.

The studio where I'd recorded my one airline ad.

We passed the old Weekly offices. One by one all those LA magazines now were bought.

There Bailey had edited and then dated and then briefly lived with a famous crime novelist. The alcoholic one who wrote *The Onyx*. She'd mentioned it in an email a few years back: How he was not to be disturbed while writing, not to be spoken to before noon. She may have even felt these terms for his writing day were her own. She may

143

even have held him to them.

Her recent hope, she'd said on the phone, was to end her career at the *LA Times*, where they took her away from personal writing and made her an editorial page assistant. They'd stationed her at the conference tables where the presidential candidates came and answered questions, enshrined her as the ecumenical holdover, the apolitical one who wanted to talk about which candidates were genuine and which were not.

It was remarkable that people like us had made a living, admitting right away that mine never looked like one. Somewhere in a storage pod was my set of faded galleys from *The New Yorker*, my nearest miss, bumped for coverage of a war in Kosovo. For years, I'd have said I wouldn't want to go to heaven if you couldn't take old galleys with you.

Philip and I found a Trader Joe's at Third and La Brea, however challenging a parking lot that portended in rush hour. What once had been a gas station had become a mansard roofed mini-mall until it couldn't bear the congestion. Now this. Parking was on two levels behind a storefront built out to the street. Drivers in Mercedes and BMWs and just-washed Toyota Highlanders zipped past you against the arrows. One had the unmellow sense of city life as the test of one's devotion.

At the freezer aisle we got stuck, because no dessert looked thoughtful or creative enough—everything too large or in need of thawing or too branded (Ho Ho's! Gone Bananas!). But Philip wanted to try the chocolate covered banana slices, so I said what the hell and bought both. Bailey would be unafraid to get some kind of kick out of them.

Which she did—a superfluous, bonus smile spreading—right after gawking at Philip's height. I always had the benefit of the doubt with Bailey.

———

Coincidences lurk in the grass for anyone who wants to find

them. She played us an LP by The Czars—the very name that Nola and I loved attaching to Philip. The album title was *The Ugly People Versus the Beautiful People*—which is basically Philip's manifesto, in a phrase.

Philip's dull smile, years later as I write this, says that any possible fondness for cosmic coincidences wore off for him a long time ago.

For dinner she served some kind of Moroccan soup, I think, or some other item that sounds not enough to serve on its own but turns out to be plenty to eat, and we ate kind of reflectively, because the songs on that Czars' album were so woozy, right up Philip's alley, gorgeous sorts of requiems to romantic enslavement. A lead vocalist's murmuring voice is tuned up louder than the madness of his whole band in full distortion, as if he's locked himself in the bathroom away from a drunken party.

"How do you always stay so current!" I asked Bailey.

Bailey laughed. "Everything I have, people send me! I know nothing! That's my darkest secret in life."

"I believe you. Not that you know nothing, but that it's your biggest secret. Bailey has no dark side," I told Philip, who joined me on her deep white sofa.

Her living room was generously spare. The sofa faced the arched front windows that opened—no matter the weather, no matter how windy or cold—onto the dark street. Bailey's reading chair faced across us to the turntable atop a simple Danish black wood table. On the Ottoman, a half dozen issues of *The Oxford American* were so evenly stacked they looked cemented, and Bailey angled her legs away from the magazines instead of the other way around. The hallway to the bedroom, just like in the old days, was lined with towers of books, as if they were overflow, but in fact they were all the books there were. All her canvases, behind the sofa, leaned against the walls unhung. Why this transitory state felt so homelike to me I never knew.

"I told you the story, right?" she said. "About the blind date who said 'ask me anything'?"

"That's why I mentioned it. You asked him if he had a dark side."

"The guy told me this awful thing," she explained to Philip. "And it was so shocking I couldn't talk to him after that."

"But you never told me what it was," I said.

"I know. I still can't!"

"You see—this is where you really confuse me."

"I can't explain!" she said. But I think she liked being this object of confusion.

"But you've always been someone I look up to, because sort of nothing is alien to you."

"No, it's—" She was thoughtful.

"*Everything* is alien to you?"

"Ha."

"Not even a category? You won't tell us his *category* of human deviance?"

She seemed to consider it, then looked as surprised as any of us by the wall she kept running into. "Nope. I really can't." No one could refuse a thing as easily as Bailey.

She rose and returned to her turntable. "Do you want old or new, Philip?"

Philip said he was neutral, but Bailey enjoyed how many of her albums he already knew and admired. There were the White Stripes and the Pixies and Louis Armstrong, whose profundo literally terrified Philip as a small child, so we started there. The ragtime recording was so old the percussion sounded like pots and pans.

Then she got momentum. We listened to a series of progressively more daring singers of indeterminate gender—successors, Bailey speculated, to Prince or Freddie Mercury—and while these tracks played, she sat back looking happy and ravished.

"What do you hear from Cody Castille?" I asked.

"Nothing since he took up with that folk singer. But I'd given up on him long before."

I exhaled—the thought of Bailey writing off anyone gave me a chill. "I know he's doing a blog now. As a lot of retired newsies are, and nobody's reading them. They should disable the comment-counters. But in Cody's case it's all reruns. 'The Time I Interviewed Muddy Waters.'"

"Can't get myself to care. Just knowing the sorts of things he did to Dehlia."

"Do you hear from—her?" The phonograph's rocker arm lifted, as if my heart had produced a skip.

"No. I always assumed you had."

I'd looked Dehlia up plenty of times, of course. She had become an academic at a community college up north. Her faculty page was an avalanche of jargon. "I'm worried irrelevance isn't kind to our generation."

"Or irrelevance is freedom. I was born to be irrelevant." Bailey laughed.

"Bailey's on the acknowledgements page of half the books in this apartment," I assured Philip.

"Seriously, if I could, I'd never go out. Door Dash everything." But she was looking at Philip. "What are you taking besides humanities, Philip?"

He looked at me, as if for a cue. "Film history?"

"From what I can tell, it's any movie his professor wants the students to see."

"I got an A on one essay," Philip said, "but my dad helped edit."

"Hardly," I said. I bragged a little about his writing. Something about how he'd described a movie's title font as reinforcing the theme of a "jet-set façade."

But Philip's eyes, I now saw, had closed.

"We got up early today," I admitted. Night air had filled the room.

"Should we serve the—what are they called?" Bailey said. "The Hoo Hoos?"

"Jesus! Only you'd get away with saying that."

"What are they called!"

"Ho Ho's! And Gone Bananas!"

And we were laughing like stoned people.

"You still want chocolate bananas, don't you, Philip?"

While we got out dishes for the dessert, Bailey prepared three cups of decaf coffee. She had read somewhere that you should wet the grounds first, but she checked with me, in case that wasn't so. Against

147

all odds, she still assumed I knew more about everything than I do.

We sipped from mismatched cups, standing in her kitchen, and then, of course, three became an odd number. Philip was leaning the wrong way against her sink, elbows before him, as if he were lecturing to her cabinets.

I excused myself to use the bathroom, and I listened while she bagged some review copies of books for Philip in the hall—that was a torch-passing for you. I know that was my wish. That somehow he could stand where I stood in 1985, feeling appreciated by her, feeling like the most exciting future was ahead, however complicated or challenging the world might become.

Of the two of us, I think, Bailey always felt like the younger one, the one who vowed never to marry or have kids, but when we hugged our goodbye, I was worrying like a child about whether I had what it took to go off alone to my own situation.

———————

"What I remember is you both snickering at me," Philip will say, years later, when I prompt him for memories. "Because of my embarrassing use of the word façade. That's why I closed my eyes."

"Wow, Philip, I can swear it wasn't snickering. Maybe fawning? Maybe we were marveling?"

He ponders my interpretation. But he by no means looks upset. He is at our breakfast table eating a huge apple fritter, because sugary calories are what Philip wakes up for in the morning. If he's having a bad thought-week, he'll say the apple fritter is the only thing. And when he wants something enough, he goes out into the wars of the world to get it.

"I also remember her advising us that we should buy lots of expensive clothes."

That I can picture Bailey saying. With her artist's eye she would have tried to persuade us that we looked elegant or aristocratic or some such thing.

But he adds, "Probably because I was dying."

"Did you say 'dying'?"

I've gotten good at not using a tone that puts him down.

"You really want me to talk about it?"

"Of course I do!"

It's not always so clear, anymore, if my son is having bad thoughts. But it helps him to talk freely, and sadly the connection helps me too. "I had looked at pornography," he begins, with the air of someone who's long been defined by one tragic mistake. "And it ruined my life. She knew that—obviously. Didn't she?"

He's always just this close, he seems to think, to a theory that explains where It All Went Wrong.

"I remember you worrying about pornography. Here's what I wonder if you mean. Any cheap habit can make us feel like we've betrayed our better instincts. And when we're conflicted, it affects how we carry ourselves. Does that kind of say it? That's such a normal thought."

He neither agrees nor disagrees, or even seems to process what I've said, before going on. "My looks were fading, just when I was becoming... leonine." This could be word blocking, one of Philip's symptoms. Or it could be the word *leonine* has come to mean something big or supernatural for him, another symptom. "Like the photo of your first wedding," he adds.

Wolfish, does he mean? I see how you could get from there to leonine.

"Anyway, I looked at pornography, so. That happened to me."

"Then why wouldn't it happen to everybody?"

He'd already anticipated the question. "Because I was rough with myself."

"You were on Prozac, Philip. So, of course, it took more—"

"Yeah, that's a real nice excuse."

If my son would just trust me completely—because honestly, we're closer to that insanity than to no trust at all—then I could tell him he's merely deep, or that he thought so highly of Bailey that he imagined she saw his secrets. Or that he takes on the world's secrets, like an empath, because such people exist. It might all be degrees.

149

After a pause, he says, "This is really helpful to you?"

"Totally."

"I was too young to be seeing what I was seeing. But I was becoming a man. At the Seal Beach library, I was at a reading table, and a woman looked at me and said, *This is a place for children*."

How I wish psychoanalysts were back in vogue. And that everyone was provided a free one: a Freudian, sailing the rivers of the psyche—like F. Scott Fitzgerald's Doctor Diver, or like our friend Steven Aldercott, staying up nights to unlock the poetry of my son's lifelong shame.

Instead Philip goes it alone. Twenty-seven years old, he is guarded enough that none of his countless fears are apparent unless you ask. And then only if you ask with no agenda. Because if you blame him for the insults he reports, or fail to take his side, he cannot bear it, least of all from a parent, nor can he bear the guilt you feel about failing him. So he learns to step outside the classroom when he's stressed, to say shush! to his thoughts beneath his breath, to shop for vintage shirts on Retro Row. Wave from the passenger seat to the local girl whose band he sometimes follows.

I ask what else he recalls about Bailey's.

"Just that all this was going on, and it made me this unattractive dog. But you didn't know."

"You weren't unattractive. And of course I didn't know."

"A person who's alone gets weird. I had no friends. You spent so much time with me, Dad, but you could never get me on track. At least you got lucky with Daniel. Daniel is the whole package."

"Philip. If you only knew. Everyone struggles."

"Things could have gone either way from that night forward. I was too young to live in my own shed. I was running when I should have been walking."

It goes without saying who encouraged him to run.

"You're probably tired of hearing about this," he says.

At Casey's, he started keeping later hours. He would pace in the lighted shed as he orbited each new misunderstanding with Lucinda, and he began complaining, first to her and then to me, about hearing other, male, voices on the line. For example, the teenaged son of the pool man from church. He felt sure of it.

He began toting a David Foster Wallace novel, *Broom of the System*, and trying to decode its hidden patterns, much like one of the too-smart-but-never-smart-enough characters might, which for Philip was like trying to swallow the LA River and spit it into mason jars. "Can I get your opinion on this chapter?" he asked. "I can't tell if it was meant to mess with readers."

I had no patience for reading the chapter. But I could answer at a glance: "*No. And yes. Because that's what literature does.* If it makes you feel upset, for goodness sake, read something else."

He slung his backpack to the leg of Casey's coffee table, by the sofa where I sat checking phone messages, and said he couldn't wait for the semester to end. A professor had mocked him.

"He probably likes you," I said. "I always tease my favorites."

But he wasn't listening. My datebook lay open on the table, and there was a sticky note attached, which Philip peeled off, then slapped down upon the table. "Why did you write that word?"

"What word?" The note was upside down from where I sat. No armadas? *"No agendas!"*

"Agendas!" he yelled. "I thought of that word today."

"Philip," I said, with my flip phone to my ear. "Words are words. No one owns them. We'll be late."

I was listening to a voicemail from Zooey, my daughter. Wanda telling her to wrap it up. Wanda feeding words. Zooey reciting, "We're going to the marathon Sunday, so Mom says to tell you we might be late." Rustling of phone. *"We're going to watch Doug,"* Zooey adds in a whisper, then Wanda yells, "Come back and tell your father you love him," but I'd snapped my phone shut.

We stepped outside. My car stood across the street, and the street looked astonishingly wide.

My mistake was trying to smile. My mistake was thinking of those

151

songs where people say to "smile on through the rain," but this made me feel more vulnerable, not less: blindfolded, or forgotten like kids whose parents forget to pick them up at school, and as I stuck the key into the ignition my breath dropped out in a kind of freezing gasp.

"I'll be okay," I choked. "Things are hard." But I continued to shake. He was going to need an explanation. "You're an adult. Almost. Wanda is dating someone," I said. "It just hurts."

Philip balled up his hands and pressed them against his eyes.

"Please, it's not your worry, Philip. I'm sorry. No one should see their dad like this."

But as his head rose a slow wail of frustration rose with him, like an attenuated note from a balloon.

"Philip!" I said. "I'll be okay."

"It's not you," he said. "It's something I saw."

I looked around.

He said, "On TV. A commercial that targeted me."

"You mean, like, demographically," I said after a moment.

"Stop always making me explain everything! It's in the textbook. They watch us."

"Maybe Google maps—maybe Internet ads. Location services."

"Mom understands."

"I think you're conflating some things."

Of course I could picture Nola mixing hippie politics with the science page of the *New York Times*.

"You never understand."

"I might be agreeing with you, Philip. I'm just—the distinction is important. Do you understand this is important?"

"Stop yelling!"

"I think we're saying the same thing. I'll drop it."

Maybe this was his intent. In an instant I was the grownup again, and he was the child. I should never have cried in his sight. His eighteenth birthday was just days ahead.

"You haven't told me if you want people over," I said.

"I don't really have friends."

"Even just Mom and Ronan. We could have a small family party."

But right before they were to arrive, he became obsessed with a certain traumatic dinner argument from many years before—in which, from what I could make out, Nola had banished Ronan to his room without supper. Philip strained to describe it, the unjustness of this memory, and I actually felt a little hopeful that he was telling it, as if this were the boil at last. If Nola's temper used to scare me, why not him?

But it was troubling to observe that he couldn't explain why the incident was so traumatic. He could only keep aping the words "Go to your room! Go to your room!" and hope he'd made his point.

I snuck off and phoned Nola—whose car was minutes away—to warn her things were fragile, and the birthday party took place under the strain of our masked concern. Nola prompted Philip several times to say how it felt to turn eighteen. Ronan piped in with stumper questions about computer languages. When I darkened the lights to bring the cake, Philip opened his gifts without joy. A wristwatch and wooly sweater from Nola. From Ronan an electric razor. A vintage typewriter from me. "The ribbon will arrive by mail," I said. I don't know if he heard me.

Casey had emerged from her room to join the birthday song, and Hao-Yu wandered in too, with a giftwrapped book. But all the awkwardness drove us to Philip's shed, where he sat himself on the edge of his bed.

"Look at me, all grown up."

"You are," Nola said. "You are all grown up."

While Ronan studied the unusable toilet and the construction of the shelves, Nola's eyes went from mine to some serious point in space, back and forth. Then she said to Philip, "I know I sometimes feel better if I can talk to someone. Like a doctor. If I'm not feeling right, I call Kaiser."

"If you want me to. But it won't help anything."

We called. A Germanic-sounding doctor on duty wanted to order a "small dose of Abilify," an antipsychotic, as if we were fools, as if we'd never read a newspaper, as if we weren't educated in the horrors of such pills, as if our son were someone else's son, and we shouted our refusal in unison.

So we opted for Plan B—an increased Prozac dose—but in the days ahead, it amped Philip up. Night after night, I tried to assure him that insomnia didn't kill anyone. But did it? Then a serious rupture. A jealous outburst. Pounding the hood of Lucinda's mother's car.

"He should be on Abilify," repeated the Germanic doctor, who seemed to take little pleasure in his certainty.

With his first dose we hiked Beachwood Canyon. I was his stoner buddy, waiting to see him come on. Palm fronds shifted in a warm breeze.

"Honestly, Philip," I said. "I'm hopeful." My newest magical thought was that the five-milligram dose would thread some mythic needle for being just enough to make Philip the best he'd ever been, and possibly even better, but not enough to make him lumber or drool. "How are you feeling now?"

He felt like buying shoes, he said—not a feeling precisely, but it was something to do. On Sunset, he almost bought a glam pair of boots that would give Elton John pause. He also asked a clerk if he could mix and match from different colors.

I got him out of that store, and we drove to American Apparel, where he spoke of a girl in film class who'd worn "balloons on her shoes," by which Philip might have meant painted-on balloons, or literal balloons, or something metaphorical. He planned to describe them in his next paper for the class.

The following Tuesday, on a visit to Nola's, he stole baked goods off a table at a Farmers Market—then admitted he'd been cheeking his pills. When we confronted him, Philip spat the afternoon dose in my face, then pleaded good humor. "It's a joke!" he protested.

The next doctor was a dashing optimist in private practice. Doctors like these have the fatherly gift of getting you to pretend, while you're with them, that you share their jolly nature, so you'll deserve their time. Their offices are near the Los Alamitos Race Track, luxurious but always changing hands, bathroom keys dangling on giant paddleboards. The new prescription was Risperdal, which made Philip woozy within minutes, so I let him nap in the maid's room at Dr. Steven Aldercott's while I got myself a soda from the fridge. "We'll be fine," I said to Steve, sitting down, and he gave me his reverent, empathetic laugh.

But Philip padded in after only a moment.

"I'm not able to sleep," he said.

"That's all right, kiddo. Should we drive back to Silver Lake? Do you want a cold drink?"

For some reason it struck me as moving to think that even in Philip's shoes one might only need a cold drink.

He looked at me, earnestly. His brashness crumbling. "Do you think we could go for a walk?"

"Happily," I said. "I would love for us to go for a walk."

I always wonder: Does he feel it too, the gypsy permanence of us when we walk? It is the reticence of all the suburban homes and our freedom from living in them. Or is it exile? I'd probably overvalued it. I probably raised him with an unhealthy idea of our uniqueness.

At the corner was a mailbox, and in my sport coat pocket was the signed consent to divorce. Here was as good a place as any to mail it. As if to afford me a private moment, Philip held back, waiting.

And then that, was done.

"I have to share something," he said when I returned to his side.

"Anything."

"First I need you to turn off your phone."

"What do you mean?"

"I don't want us to be interrupted."

"Phone off," I said. It was a blessed thing to be asked to do. I felt grateful.

"I'm going to kill you," he said.

"Come again?"

One more time—he could just tell—he'd been desperately misunderstood. "Don't worry! I got the message! I'm going to kill you."

I calmed myself, as I began to think a few things through.

"The message. I'm letting you know I got it." Now he looked

155

less certain.

"How were you thinking of doing it?"

"Smother you with a pillow?"

"Philip," I began, forgetting that my father's calm tone has always backfired, and when Philip sensed the disconnection, I reached for my phone.

"You promised!"

"I'm concerned, Philip, and so I'm calling Mom."

He ran.

"Philip, I'm concerned!" I yelled, giving chase, and after a block he slowed, tiring, but as I neared he made his break again.

"I'm not going to let you get away."

"I can't go to a hospital. Promise me."

"Come to the car!" I was panting.

"What did I do? I didn't do anything!"

"Do you realize? Philip, we'll get help."

"Promise no hospital."

"Get in the car," I repeated.

Why did he comply? Perhaps he was winded. Perhaps, like a kitten seeing the outdoors for the first time, he lacked the imagination to run away from me.

We made it to the 605, and then, with a burst of almost giddy curiosity, Philip raked at the steering wheel. I slapped his hand away as we swerved across two lanes of the freeway. He grabbed the wheel again, and I prayed to God out loud; this made Philip laugh at me, and he sat back in peace, either defeated or inexplicably victorious, all the way to the ten-day hold in Kaiser-Chinatown.

It was not, looking back, the worst of Philip's hospital stays.

He kissed a girl there. A student of the Cordon Bleu. A better class of patient than he'd encountered that time at Cerritos. They showed each other their printed diagnoses.

Locked down, he was briefly himself.

There were two weeks of daily aftercare, which we tried to normalize by flinging Frisbees in the parking lot each morning.

But on a new antipsychotic—his third, already, and there'd be others—all his bravado fell away. Only meekness and trepidation now. We moved his mattress to Casey's living room, with her blessing, but everything around us said our time was up.

———————

One detail of our leaving Silver Lake seems significant.

I'd been ruining my haircut with a razor ever since just before the meeting with the elders of my former church. Not having liked it the morning of. If you have an alcoholic mind, you should never cut hair. Leave alone whether it is wise that you have children. On our last night in Silver Lake, after Philip had swallowed his meds and fallen asleep on the mattress in the living room beside my chair bed, it felt plain to me that the world would be a gentler place if only my hair would lie down.

The occupant to ask, of course, was Hao-Yu. You see the opportunist that I am—you are gay, you must cut hair—but the thought of revealing myself as a jerk did zero to deter me. If anything, it made my request feel more needful and pure.

So long as I would submit my embarrassment to Hao-Yu, and—this seemed important—refuse to judge the result, and—one more stipulation—have him cut the hair wet—*then*, it felt clear to me, I'd be prepared for all the challenges that Philip and I would face in the months ahead.

And Hao-Yu agreed (yes, he cut hair, but only rarely), although it was already late at night, and his carefulness made it much later. To this day I can feel the solemnness of Hao-Yu's concentration. I can feel the horror of my tired face—how long since I'd been young?—softened by the calmness of Hao-Yu's work. It was long after midnight when I went to my chair bed, anxious to lay my forehead onto the pillow while Philip snored, and wanting the hair never to dry.

———————

I also went to my valise, because of course the time had come to throw away the picture of my wife. But I searched in the folds now and it was gone, or I'd moved it, and—anyway. I was much too tired to remember what I'd done with it, much too tired to think. But I could rest, now, because I was free of Wanda's picture.

———————

When a loved one is ill, family history gets asked about, and memories come back like a familiar old infection.

For example, during my own parents' divorce, when I was five or six, I'd started seeing things at night. Groups of phantoms had paced my bedroom, as if turning a millstone.

And yet the paralysis I remember feeling—and knowing that the zombies' business did not intersect with my own except in a certain theater defined only by space and not time—for some reason opened a prairie of supernatural calm for me. If I screamed for my parents, this clearing in the center of fear would be taken away. As long as I didn't scream, the zombies, although scary, were my own.

This is a perspective I'm lucky enough, at some instants, to be granted. That off switch to fear that I've spoken of. Perhaps no one's demons have to, or ought to, frighten anyone else. Perhaps anyone's demon is everyone's. We're together in all this, is what I mean, even when physically we're not.

It mangled me, my parents' divorce, but it's also who I am, and it can provide a certain overarching, exotic view in the presence of my enemies.

Maybe I mistook that war correspondent's coldblooded stare on the cover leaf of the book from Dr. Steven.

Often when I remember our time in Silver Lake, Philip and I are hashing things out on one of our walks around the reservoir. The lake itself is Edenic but a backdrop, a peacefulness glimpsed through wrought iron. Wholeness, temptation and exile, in a single glance.

And as we circle, we remind me of silent comedians, beating water out of our hats. *Whose fault is it, this fine mess?* we might be asking each other, with raised voices.

But no one else on the trail can seem to see or hear our phantasmic commotion.

Philip and I moved back to Long Beach on April 29, 2011, a fact I wouldn't mention except that every year Facebook resurrects a photographic "memory" from the same day one year earlier: my photo of the moon in the hole of the Angel Food Donut. In other words, our story encompassed one full trip around the sun. If, Cape Canaveral-like, it followed that we'd now reached the perfect astral window to try our luck leaving Long Beach again, we had very little heart to.

In those days, of course, the question of whether Philip would "recover" seemed the only question worth asking. At a later stage, it was whether hoping was a trap.

And even later there'd be days when I had the otherworldly sense that all would be well in the by and by, although of course that feeling never visits for as long as you would like.

Grant us, Lord, not to be anxious about earthly things, but to love things heavenly; and even now, while we are placed among things that are passing away, to hold fast to those that shall endure.

There were the colorful attempts to go med-free. A local vegan restaurant let Philip wash dishes while he lived in the car that he'd bought with his college fund so Social Security wouldn't take it away. A young waitress burned him a beloved CD. He spent one golden afternoon with her skinny-dipping at Malibu, first driving by Lucinda's house to yell vengeful taunts. All that landed him back at Chinatown. He phoned me to retrieve the CD from his car—and I did, but I played every song on it first, reclining in the driver's seat and absorbing the tobacco-and-ocean smell of his summer's laundry.

But as curious as I am for more details of Philip's one briefly happy summer, and though I've begged him to write down his recollections, he won't. He gives me three reasons, depending on the day.

1. His stories are too personal.
2. His stories are so personal they're sacred.
3. His stories are so sacred they're taboo. He'll be condemned to hell for speaking of them.

(My feeling now is that these explanations differ only by degrees of abstraction. So at what point is any of them to be judged unsound?)

Thus, a lot of Philip's first summer as an adult is unknown to me. I did see him build an Ikea bed with his own hands, demanding that I let Lucinda move in and share it. I did get collection notices for an unpaid parking ticket in San Francisco. I did hear him beg me to write some stories about the 1980s in Los Angeles and about Bailey Kavanagh.

Whom I got to see that summer for dinner at a popular restaurant in Beverly Hills.

It was because of an interesting book idea she'd come up with, in which all her favorite feature writers would contribute maga-zine-style profiles of Bailey herself. This in order for her to interject commentary about the vanishing craft that she'd always championed (while claiming to be baffled by it).

Not a bad idea! And with all those great writers I'd looked up to when I was young! Although I more than half suspected my inclu-sion was based on pity, that it was Bailey's way of helping me rehabil-itate myself as a writer.

She was at the far end of the darkened bar and I found her by the shape of her hair cut high on the back of her neck, the bangs slightly too high across her forehead—Bailey's bangs always looked five min-utes short of comfortable, but that was the fashion. Nothing but neck and forehead in the dark above a shiny black jersey. The once blue hair from her days at the Masque was now just long and conventional enough to point down, not up. But her skin was still cryogenically dewy (she would call it fat girl sweat), perhaps (I liked to think) because of the anti-aging properties of a life spent keeping other people's imagi-nations young. Childless, childlike. Complete and uncompleted.

We took a booth where I played reporter and asked about the highlights of her career, and heard again her stories about the West Coast days and the amazement she'd never stopped feeling at the realization that people really and truly were being paid to have that much fun. And all the unforgettable articles she'd edited about pot-addicted teens and child-molesting sitters and Mexico in the air, and jai alai and dog races and Quaaludes and busing and water politics and smog and pot farms. And that time, at the *Washington Post*, when she'd woken up David Remnick in Russia to ask about a comma.

And the big brains who loved her openness, and those who didn't, one of whom asked, when she fact-checked the name of an important politico, if she "even was sentient."

All through this she fingered a big glass half full of white wine, a watery platinum, which she claimed she must be feeling because she was talking so much. She said she had a headache and I thought I could see it turn her face into a slab of effort when she laughed her pleasured laugh. What neither of us said: "It's a nostalgia volume, isn't it?"

When we left the restaurant, she told me a dream she'd had about Philip: He had approached her, Bailey said, with the important-seeming but cryptic message: "I've seen a lot."

What could this mean? she wanted to know.

And I could only guess, but how does a father who's lived so chaotically, for all his attempts to be more present than his own father, not hear himself indicted by those words?

In the weeks after that dinner, I created file after file of notes, preparing the kind of story Bailey Kavanagh would love while immortalizing Bailey Kavanagh. But whenever I tried to write passages, her essence eluded me, and all I ever finished was the query.

Not that I'm certain the other contributors came through with anything more than that.

She even insisted on paying for my time on the profile: a thousand-dollar advance. It being the recession, and me having lost that family house, and her having no children to feed. To which I replied, in an email, that such charity was out of the question, but she pushed back, saying she wished she could give every artist friend of hers some money without strings. Here she was earning good money and no one to support. And she sounded heartfelt enough that for a little while, I felt like a deserving young writer again, privileged to write things or never write them, saying yes to both her encouragement and her gift.

Museum of Art: 2019

—◆—

Bailey Kavanagh sends Richard Leviton by text message four short audio clips, which he opens from his phone in a university parking lot after a marathon evening class.

In each clip she recites, in a cool, intimate monotone, random phrases that she's transcribed while listening to TV news. He turns his collar to the evening mist as he presses the phone close.

Old enough at sixty-four to have sat through plenty of ironical, uninflected performance-art things, old enough to have thought it new and exciting to hear John Lennon defamiliarizing dance names through his nose on Revolution 9 (*"The Watusi"*. . . *"The Twist…"*), Leviton infers that Bailey's project intends to arrest him with the almost erotic meaninglessness and isolation of their times. Not to mention his son's familiar nemesis, The Culture.

Except, hearing her voice, now, he finds himself not saddened by the times but instead transported to a secret cathedral in the heart of it.

Was it voices, all along, for him? He tries to replay in his head the sounds of the significant voices from his younger life, and finds that this is amazingly easy to do.

And he's envious, although not in an unpleasant way, of how much artists like Bailey can achieve saying so little, while writers achieve so little by saying so much—well.

It's been a long teaching day, and he's so tired that anything will sound like an oasis from this parking lot. Tired enough nowadays that he can begin to feel grateful to be replaced. *Your stories are the ones that need to be heard,* he'll say to his first-generation students, who look twelve. Grandstanding, a little, yet his voice swells up with real feeling.

But he will go home and share the clip with his 27-year-old son, who will nod and say, "I was just thinking about Bailey!"

———

On vacation with Philip, Leviton tours the San Diego Museum of Art and finds himself weeping in unashamed wonder. Leviton, who'd been tone-deaf to paintings!

He chokes up before a Roger Kuntz of a living room in Laguna. Where did the 1960s go? And how is it you can recognize them just by the interior light?

In the Spanish Masters exhibit, he cries before *The Penitent Saint Mary Magdalene.* Then *The Virgin Mary as a Child, Asleep*—it's the dramatic irony, he guesses, that undoes him: the future we know that the painted child can't. And this the painter captures by... omission? Leviton won't ever explain it: It's the unspeakably consequential future that awaits every child unawares. Our minds are too small to hold this.

———

What the twenty-first century needs, Leviton decides one day, is better wallet cards. *He is shy. No paramedics, please. Adopt this neighbor as your own.*

Leviton's son enters the living room, flops on the couch, sighs, curses, leaves, and returns until the father explodes from his desk: "Will you ever stop advertising your pain?"

The son shouts, "I'm sorry! I guess my brain needs sustenance!"

"Yes, it does! So go find some!"

"Will you stop yelling? It's so predictable!"

"Yes, it's predictable! I'm predictable! I'm a B-list writer! I need all the concentration I can get!"

The son says nothing.

"I'm going to Cafe Windsor!" the father continues.

"Bye, Dad," his son replies—and not at all in the foghorn tone that he sometimes deploys for rudimentary guilt. It's as innocent a good-bye as the father thinks he's ever heard—so absent any blame, while no less saddened.

The echo of the father's exasperation hangs like a suit of clothes for Goodwill, and there'll be no way in the father's lifetime he'll ever learn to thank the bigger party in the heat of a dispute, but he does so later with his apology, and Philip thanks him too.

———

Instead of the regular visit from the young social worker, Alicia—who the father wishes would spend less time chatting about popular bands and more time teaching Philip how to balance life chores with play, or how to sit on a bus without acting like you're being pelted by spit wads—her agency today is hosting for its disabled clients a TeleStar! Awards Ceremony at a banquet hall near the JCC. There, Philip, who has maintained a 4.0 average at the community college, will be honored with a trophy for Education. Leviton is welcomed to attend, but he has his own full day of classes to teach. Philip is welcomed to prepare a speech, but it's also totally fine if he doesn't.

Of course even the handshake on the dais could require some planning, for a boy who could never properly lie. A boy who thinks the "selves" that other grownups carry into banquet rooms are somehow more real than his own, a boy who thinks his own options are limited to either unpardonable honesty or unpardonable artifice.

"It's like I have no self," he'll sometimes explain, to which the father sometimes jokes, "You know they call that Nirvana."

But it's a Nirvana that's left this exiled son still panicked by what to wear. The jeans have a coppery dinge. The shirt collar is rolled under on one side. The nice brogues look kind of stuck on, too—although, the overall effect could pierce the right audience, Leviton thinks, remembering how it felt so long ago to keep trying to hide his socks beneath the cuffs of his khakis at Cody Castille's.

Leviton says, and his voice goes hoarse, "Philip, I know you think this award is some kind of a joke, and I know you will do greater things. But you earned this. Hear me please. What you've battled through. Take this in."

After some apparent puzzlement over which reaction will get this moment to pass, Philip chooses out of nowhere an expression of outright sensibility. "Okay!" he decides.

He is hiding his teeth in a smile, because he hates his teeth, but it's a smile.

How the non-speech goes, Leviton doesn't hear, because Philip is so worn out upon return. So they go to their respective corners.

It's near bedtime when Philip emerges for milk and meds.

"Bobby's given up on me," he says.

Bobby is a high-school reacquaintance, a high-functioning autistic, somewhat bossy in his opinions—but, as the father has pointed out, a friend—an actual friend!—within today's loose, social-media definition of the word. Tonight one of the boy's online rants triggered Philip, who replied, *You sound like my enemies.*

Leviton weighs this crisis. "I bet it's fixable."

"Unless they really got to him."

"They?"

A long silence. "I guess that might be paranoia," Philip says.

———

Sundays, they attend an Episcopal church. Or Richard attends, while Philip stations himself on a folding chair in the empty social hall with a novel to read. Over months, years, he becomes recognized, then accepted, then warmly regarded by the mostly AOL-generation congregants who stream in for muffins and coffee after the service. He learns to converse, to ask skillful questions.

Ever so slowly the kind of young adulthood Philip has envied and yearned for becomes too young for him—an age-inappropriate yearning. He has slumbered through a rite of passage that no longer will realistically excite him. He would stick out at a college party not for his awkwardness but his seriousness.

He could arrive fully formed at age thirty to a new city, attend university, but if they ask what he did with his twenties, he would need some help planning the words.

"Say you tried to be a writer. You suffered a post-traumatic anxiety disorder and you learned to live with it. And it gave you a weird maturity and immaturity rolled into one. This is me talking now. Maybe life hasn't been a straight line."

Leviton feels sometimes that he's training a secret agent. And as he does so, the names of faraway cities the father is too old to romanticize take on a naïve, vicarious promise again: Seattle, Champagne-Urbana, Omaha.

Also, the father notices, when the Sunday regulars fail to reciprocate with friendly conversational questions for Philip, it's often on them. It's ordinary gracelessness. The son is rebuffed only in the same way just about everyone is by the 2010s.

But once in the car, taxed by an hour's interactions, Philip seethes to Richard and Daniel and Zooey about his social failures all the way home.

On the dining room table, Leviton finds a Who Am I questionnaire that Philip has completed for the social worker. *I've been successful at: My last two semesters of school. I will reach my goals because I am: Studious. I am loved by: Mom and Dad.*

Leviton's eye moves past the inevitable blank lines. (*I like myself because:___ I'm an expert at_____ I have a natural talent for:_____*) and sees this:

The person I admire most is: My dad.

Leviton's first thought is a kind of reverent alarm. *How would a better man receive this.* He looks like George Bush reading to school-children on 9-11, after the aide has whispered something in his ear.

The bombshell is inconveniently timed. Something to live up to, just when Leviton has reached an age when he longs to be less nice in every way.

Add to this Leviton's awareness that his son probably admires him for things that Leviton no longer admires. Like being a more employable but inarguably more bogus version of his son; like knowing what to say a good deal of the time.

He does feel proud that he hadn't sent Philip to board and care, that summer when the Gables shut down. All those overmedicated souls gazing from the windows. But Leviton can't judge those other families' choices. For him there'd been so much luck involved.

What amazes him is that amid a staggering paranoid illness, his son has chosen at key moments to believe someone who loves him—imagine this. For someone with a paranoid psychosis to trust in someone else's reality, a reality that's opposite his own mind! What a thin reed to clutch! How had he done it? Was it grace? Was it God? And if so, why so little of it!

Amazement at ordinary heroism—that's another thing that fools like Leviton come to feel. At an age when nothing else feels good, why does it feel so good to feel pain?

How glad Leviton is that he never cried his last tear!

———————

What a cough Philip had when they'd landed this apartment. *E-hu, E-hu,* all through the night, like some biblical lament. Then listing over the wood floor, the vomit dropping to the floor before it warned of coming up. That did it for Leviton, and on Philip's new med they'd been told to watch for embolism. So they headed to the ER. But Leviton parked timidly in a long-term structure, thinking it much closer to Admissions than it was. It had to have been a mile of indoor corridors with painted arrows: Leviton navigating, pale Philip straggling behind.

Naturally, the CT showed widespread pneumonia—aspiration variety, a permanent hazard of nighttime drooling. Naturally they caught it barely in time. Naturally the hospital bed at full extension was comically short for a man of 6'4".

But for the duration of his hospital stay, watched over by his father and mother and by a series of nurses through the glass of his quarantined room, the son was more genial than at almost any time since he'd learned to walk. It wasn't just the fever, either. He joked with Leviton and Nola, a steady burble of exquisitely timed, and often nonsensical, cocktail-hour banter.

How easily he had taken to being nurtured there. How fortunate, his readiness to comply. A quality Leviton never had and never would.

———————

Ruling out the possibility of a Father's Day breakfast in the works, because he smells nothing, and because Philip most years barely scribbles a card, Leviton is doubly surprised when his son does in fact plod into Leviton's bedroom extending a plate of eggs, bacon and toast—announcing, as if Leviton's own father joylessly completing a boot camp for liberated men: "Here."

———————

On Labor Day they sit with boxed lunches beneath a tree in two facing camping chairs, the cupholder-and-canvas kind that telescope into a canvas sleeve. Right away Philip smears tomato on his favorite white t-shirt, an accident that sends Richard to the restroom to get wet paper towels. But the stain only spreads; it will have to be sprayed with Shout when they get home.

Philip, offering his unique brand of consolation, says that he'd expected to ruin the shirt anyway, and Leviton, after a slight show of how furious such resignation makes him, struggles up from the chair to weakly toss his son a football.

As if overnight, in one's middle sixties, warm-up tosses are the whole game. How high the sky seems, and how thin the air. And the new way the grassy earth seems to lift toward you on its own. It's like he's a prankster, running out onto the field of the Coliseum, only stadium security has turned on a magnetic force field that triples the Earth's gravity.

The two are mutually grateful to play, and just as grateful to drive home.

"Remember that year," says Leviton, as they pass Golden West College, "when you tried to finish out a semester here, and one night you left your notebook in class? You were so tired and overwhelmed, but a girl in class followed you outside to return your book?"

"I can barely remember," his son says. "I was just surviving."

"I know it. And that same night a stranger paid for my protein bar at Cal State, and anytime anything happened that felt lucky or kind, back then, I would feel kind of sick and well at the same time. Every day I made you an egg salad sandwich to take in your lunch and you ate it and slept on the grass between your morning class and your night class. And I would ask if it was enough for you, and you said it was. I just loved and hated how it was enough for you."

The 22 Freeway has become 7th Street, a few miles from home, and Leviton considers picking up some notes from his University office, but ultimately drives past, best to get dinner going, feed and walk the dog.

"Wow, Philip, we could have picnicked right here, at Recreation Park." Leviton's hobby now is finding the easier option. "We didn't have to go all the way to Huntington."

"I've never been to Recreation Park."

"Sure you have!" Leviton says, switching on the car radio, and as soon as he hears the tinny acoustics of a live press conference, he knows it's something terrible. A boat had thirty-five aboard when it caught fire. Only five survivors, only eight bodies found.

Leviton's breath shortens and his throat seizes up and he clicks the radio off. "I always thought age and experience made a person less sensitive. I can't filter anything anymore."

"Me neither," says Philip.

In half a year, Leviton will have heard about the spread of a "novel virus" in Wuhan, China, and all the suffering there. Would a plague reach our shores? Maybe every generation sips from that cup eventually. Maybe his generation has outrun disaster longer than most. Belatedly he'll be one with human history.

Boat fires and school shootings, on the other hand, with those live audio feeds with cameras clicking and whirring, are something different: Random, violent and obscene. It feels almost like his duty to repudiate them.

"Music then?" Leviton punches a button, and seventies pop has never sounded worse.

"Quiet is nice."

"You know what we could do for dinner?" Leviton says after a moment. "Smoothies. We haven't had smoothies since last summer."

"With the leftover Vons chicken."

"And fries."

"That sounds good," Philip says, with the unique relief he expresses when a sound next step is identified, such as fries. "And I'll text Mom. As I do every day." There is no self-criticism in this comment.

"And the new fruit bowl we ordered should be in the mail area. Amazon delivers on holidays." Leviton feels his own mood rising.

In the parking garage, Leviton carries the delivery under one arm to the elevator, scrolling a neighborhood discussion forum on his phone. *Bewear ring thiefes.* "No one can spell," he grumbles, "even in the wealthy part of Long Beach."

"Would I have a girlfriend if I lived in LA?" Philip asks.

"Maybe. I think I'm done with cities, though. I think about the desert sometimes. Or Montrose."

The elevator bongs and a neighbor couple, black, retired, join them, which means Leviton will do the embarrassing thing where he brings strangers up to speed on the cute thing he's discussing with his son. "Where do you think a 27-year-old kid should go to live? Not that he drives me crazy or anything."

And they all laugh (Well he's a big guy, he can live anywhere he wants), then the neighbors debark on Floor 2.

"I have to get away from here soon," Philip says.

Leviton postpones this thought, or he keeps it aloft in a softer, curious way. "Where do you picture being?"

"LA, I guess. Although I've never been to Portland."

Leviton nods, unlocking their unit door. They've reached the end of summer vacation, like a Sunday times ten. It's both a sorrow and a relief to prepare their heads for the challenges of the week. "If you'll take that shirt off, I'll soak it. But you have to walk the dog for me."

After the smoothies and the fries, Philip gulps down his meds, then seats himself on the unit's west-facing couch to watch the room go dark with the sunset, one floppy hand patting the family dog. It's been a very nice apartment to them for the most part, thinks Leviton. Despite the fact no one reads in this town. Despite the vengeful music from the scavengers on bikes down below. A thankful boredom. Though already, he knows, his son strains against the boredom, just as Leviton no longer does.

Philip exchanges goodnight texts with Nola as Leviton lingers, beholding him there safe.

Double Parking at
the St. Germain: 1990

—◆—

THE DAY I MET the newcomer, he came budging four big boxes and a duffel up the ramp to the back door of the Wilshire-Plymouth meeting, stopping a couple times to straighten his back and wearing a look of industrious high hope. He had on a tan dress shirt and a bulky, wide-lapelled charcoal-colored suit jacket that implied he wanted to be seen as someone reformed. Equally at home on a yacht or in traffic court.

Of all the categories of people who depressed me that year, near the top of the list were underdogs who seemed a little too proud of what they'd been through. Jailbird preachers. Veterans with boom boxes hailing each other on my street, as if the whole world was already starting to be more theirs than mine.

I stared out the open back door. It looked more and more obvious that nobody was going to do the program thing and welcome him. Which meant no one except me was in enough emotional trouble to need to. That was depression—stunning you, always, with whatever sad truth you least could hold—and it took the air and the walls and the floor away.

"Are you the greeter, by any chance?" he said.

172

I wanted to be rude, the way certain people I admired could, people who were true to their depression. But to do that, I think you had to go all the way and give up hope. "I'm *a* greeter."

"Ah," he said. "I probably prefer that anyway."

He had two voices, I would come to learn: a super bright, adolescent one and this other one, in a lower register, that was more of a slurry, private lament. Like someone confiding bad news to his dog.

"Would it be okay if I leave my boxes in the corner there?"

"Wow, I honestly don't know. I mean, I guess they're fine." Wouldn't it have been smarter of him not to ask?

"I can't seem to throw away books. It either shows what a big brain or what a pea brain I am. Hang on a second."

He went and fished his AA Big Book from the top of one of his boxes just as someone called, "Meeting time!"

I couldn't resist cracking, "Those aren't *all* Big Books, are they?"

An awkward second passed, but then his smile wised up. "Right! That would be pretty good." And suddenly, miraculously, we seemed to be giggling together, our shoulders shaking all the way to the chairs.

"Where are you moving from, anyway? Or to?"

"I'm going to share about that," he whispered, and the meeting gavel struck.

The fact was, I had an interesting track record back then of turning the people I was supposed to be helping into my rescuers. This was in my downward spiral after Dell, the girl-wonder rock critic for *The LA Daily News*. She used to dictate concert reviews to the copy desk by pay phone while I kissed her up and down her neck—nevermore! A year later, she had decided to look into applying to law schools, with me in tow. But I was so clearly the junior partner in this plan it freaked me out, not to mention that whenever she was chasing any new ambition, she stopped wanting sex. My shocking response—in what the program called Contrary Action—had been to break up and get a solo apartment. I enlisted Rodney, my sponsee, to help me move, and watched him wobble with my queen-sized mattress across his back all the way across the parking lot to where my Mazda was; he managed one hand free to rake at the hatchback lid, my mattress slowly, slowly pinning him to the asphalt. Since that day, I had no longer been his sponsor.

Then there'd been the truck driver whose newlywed daughter, who lived in Mid-Wilshire, wouldn't let him stay on her couch during a stopover. He taught me a reconciliation prayer from a strange church pamphlet he'd picked up, about releasing all the errors of my life ("Miracles do nothing, they merely undo what never was real…"), and I prayed it—experimentally, one foot in the canoe, partly to make him think that, for a glamorous underground freelance writer from LA, I was also interestingly earnest. Pretending, ironically, to be the lost child that I actually was. But keeping one foot safely back on shore, feeling those two worlds touch.

———————

By the time he got himself called on, the meeting had gone on forever, and he made a little performance out of lowering his raised hand and rubbing out the soreness in his shoulder. He waited for the nervous laughter in the room to die out completely, prologue to his opening silence.

"I'm grateful to be sober this day," he said, and here he turned, quite dramatically, to face me. "Grateful to have made a new sober friend." I had already been hunched forward staring at the floor, so I decided it made some sense to stay that way.

"Who *are* you?" came the group's sour rejoinder.

"Wade," he said. "I'm Wade and I'm an alcoholic."

He'd arrived three days before on a bus from Denver, he said, because sobriety is full of surprises, another one being the fact that he now found himself needing to ask for a place to sleep—just two more nights while he waited for the all-clear on a room at the St. Germain Residential Apartments around the corner. It was only on the direction of his sponsor, back in Colorado, that Wade had agreed to float this humiliating request to the universe.

"And now I guess I have," he concluded—wrapping up to what sounded like healthy applause, even with a possibly adoring, murmuring backflow. A former Rolling Stones promoter leaned on his cane with eyes shut, snoring. A soap opera actress in joggers, flawless except for a jaw that always looked to me like she was sucking on a martini olive, nodded toward Wade and whispered, *Welcome*.

In our own row, a Lou Reed figure in shades lay back in his chair, marking himself off limits.

In fact, hardly any men risked looking in our direction at all, aside from the meeting's elders—who, as everybody knew, were exempt from the kind of front-line duty that included housing homeless visitors—and they were mostly laughing and nudging each other at the beauty of this sudden match: Richard and Wade, Wade and Richard.

From one row back, the famous actor Michael Hardaway said, "Is this perfect or what?" and roughly massaged the back of my neck.

This same Michael Hardaway, back when I was new, had practically jumped from his convertible downtown—I'd been on my way to traffic court, come to think of it—to yell hello to me, celebrity to nobody. I could barely believe he had the same disease as me.

"I wonder if all those AA movie stars are more emotionally evolved beings than other people, and that's what made them such talented actors in the first place." I aired this mystery to Wade— he was either a very thoughtful listener, or he had no idea what I meant. We were in my car heading to Los Feliz, the tops of palm trees listing in the haze. He had his thick suit coat folded in his lap, and, depressed though I was, I could imagine the two of us passing for world travelers. Hollywood always felt forgiving to outcasts that way. Nobody had to believe that what they saw was the finished version of you.

I managed to tell him the sad tale of my adorable rock critic, and to brag about my monthly sports column at *LA Style*, through all of which Wade seemed entertained—or, as I said, just lost.

"What about you?" I said. "What's your story? What's your dream?"

"College." It appeared to be the simplest question he'd been asked

175

in a long time. "College, but not yet."

"Really? What comes first?"

"*What comes first.*" If he didn't look so suddenly panicked, as if the tallest palm tree was about to crash onto our roof, he would have sounded menacing. "What comes first is study skills. After God and recovery, I mean. I know, this is all as simple as breathing to someone like you."

"Oh, don't be so sure," I said.

"My father had an exterminator company—the most I figured I'd ever be was his dispatcher—but my Navy recruiting officer, he was like a father. He showed me Mortimer Gadwell's series on education and he put volume one in my hand and said, 'Read me the beginning.' So I turned to page one, but the guy was all shaking his head like, *Hopeless!* He made me go back and read him *the copyright page.*"

I smirked to make sure Wade knew that I didn't like stories with punch lines.

"What do you think of Gadwell, anyway?" he asked. "Or Bennett J. Fields? Pendegrass?"

Three stupendous misses.

"This is just for two nights," I reminded him.

Outside my building, I risked getting a parking ticket so we could unload our cargo, feeding a two-hour meter and hoping I'd remember to come back.

"It's only one room," I said, raising the hatchback. "And I might have to cut things short to leave town on an assignment." This was an outright lie. "I guess I'm giving you my list. Most importantly, I'm all about quiet writing space in the mornings."

"Totally. I admire your discipline." Wade grunted as he placed a second box on the pavement on top of the first. "I'll go to the morning meeting anyway."

When my building's elevator opened at the third floor, the depression ambushed me again. It was like some kind of chloroform—I had to excuse myself while I stood there bent and gasping. You could see Wade take on the guilt, and you could see him try to deflect it.

"If my sponsor didn't keep reminding me to accept help—" His eyes had begun welling with tears.

"I know. I'm sure it will be a good thing for me," I said, straightening up slowly and fumbling for my key.

"I told my sponsor, only if it helps the other guy too. I insisted!"

"I appreciate the favor," I said, and somehow we were laughing again.

The first thing was to give him my one extra bedroll, which I finally found under my bed, but I had to look everyplace else for it first. It was nearing sundown. Wade lay down in the corner, his box tower beside him as a nightstand. My studio apartment had never looked so small. I ate a frozen Stouffer's dinner and offered him one too, but he held up a traffic-stopping palm. He did go outside, once, to have a cigarette.

When he came back, he began his nightly reading. (First book out: *You Can Be a Scholar*, which had cassette tapes attached in a pouch.) I did some reading too, because I thought I should—Jayne Anne Phillips, and a book on Zen whose cover I liked having on my coffee table in case of female visitors, because it had a sparse and sensual design that I thought made the place seem open-aired or languid. Around nine, seeing he wasn't slowing down, I turned out all the lights—maybe I had a rude side after all.

I heard the cover of his book close, a leathery thud. "I was at the end of a paragraph anyway. Although it was a really interesting paragraph." Pause. "You'd be interested. I should let you sleep."

"No." I took a fortifying breath. "I'm curious."

"All right." I saw his silhouette rise up against the window. "Actually, it kind of pertains to you."

"Pertains to me?"

"I mean, it totally pertains to you!" His voice brimmed. "It's about 'The Raven,' which is a very important poem—did the word *poetry* come from Poe, incidentally? No, of course not. At any rate, Poe apparently boasted that he wrote his poem by a process of totally mathematical induction. He deduced that if the best poem is the most profound, and the most profound subjects known to man are death and beauty, then the ultimate poem should consider as its theme the death of beauty. And then keep, you know, harkening to it. As in the refrain, 'Nevermore.' Is that incredible? You used that word yourself, earlier, in the car."

"I don't think I'd have said 'Nevermore.'"

"Some other poetic word then? 'Alas'?"

"The point is," I said, "as far as that goes, someone could claim everything we write is about the death of beauty. Since all of life is heading that direction. I don't know how remarkable this is."

"So, would you say the ideal sports column is really about death?"

Before I could venture another answer in the dark, his gotcha laugh cut me off. "Maybe you should reread Poe," he said. Then came a *click!* and his reopened book was brightened by a tiny penlight.

"Oh. Go ahead. By all means," I said, and curled myself into a ball.

Going to bed with major depression could feel like you were wearing a vest made of dynamite sticks, and every thought was a burning match. In the dark, I felt surrounded by Wade's hoary, obsolete philosophers, whom I envisioned dressed in clown collars, getting ready to haunt my dreams, or forcing me to watch old sitcoms and die drunk in the apartment.

"Will we wake up in time, do you think?" Wade said. "So I can bus to the seven o'clock meeting?"

"You ought to be fine with the east-facing window," I said, pulling the topsheet up over my shoulders. I had given him half my day. Maybe having the most meager allotment of generosity to share with others made me, in some respect, a saintlier giver than people who were born with more—like homeopathy, with the smallest dose producing the greatest recovery—this was profound, I might work it into the sports column, if I could just articulate it, if I could see the precise bicycle it was riding on, which was when I realized I'd already been asleep for a couple of hours.

In the darkness, Wade was snoring lightly.

In the amplified calm of being the last person awake, I got up and walked toward the window, where I gazed outside all alone. I heard a neighbor's bathroom fan whirr on and off; my car stood, ticketed, in the metered lot below. The coast felt clear for a minute, although who ever knew from what. I felt proprietary and proud that Wade was safe asleep.

———————

The next morning, I got straight to it, the hum of my electric typewriter rattling my card-table desk. "I wish I had your discipline," was all Wade said, putting on his suit coat.

In maybe half an hour I'd passed the magic dateline from pretending to work on my column to actually working. But when I got up from the desk to stretch, I had a vision of Wade soaking up the attention at the morning meeting, Wade being cooed over by all the same people who used to coo over me, and it upset me. As the working adult in this domestic arrangement, I felt shortchanged. I tried to remind myself that Wade had put himself in a place of terrifying limbo. Even when he smiled, he had looked near crying.

But when he got back hours later, no sooner did he shed his suit coat and unlace his shoes than I let it be known that I, too, needed a meeting. It was getting dark, which reinforced my righteousness.

If he was less than happy about being carted off to a second meeting in one day, Wade didn't show it. He washed under his arms with a green bar of cheap soap from his duffel, while I set my phone machine to answer, only this got me wondering. "The St. Germain—you gave them my number so they can reach you, right?"

Wade froze. "That wouldn't be—you know—dangerous? Letting them know that I'm in transit?"

"Writing down a phone number doesn't do that! Whose number did you put on the application?"

It was awful, the way he began to moan. "Ahhhh! The mistakes!"

"Come on, Wade. It's only one mistake that I know of. Did you give them some other number?"

"They said we'd do that after they get the place cleaned. But yes," he said, "I hear you, and like I said, you have experience that I don't. I should call right away and give them a number. Instead of dropping by after the place is cleaned. That's what you're saying."

179

"I guess I'd have thought you'd already done that."

"The management office closed at three," he said. He stood there a prolonged time. "It's moot. We're making you late now."

But in the car, nothing felt resolved.

"There's no point wallowing in this," I told him. "You said it yourself."

"I could at least have left them a voicemail."

I swerved into a service station, scraping change from the ashtray. "Which we're doing. We're doing that right now."

By the air and water bay, I eavesdropped while Wade recited within the booth: "Yes, this is for Mr. Elkins, on the vacant room?" It was not a bad beginning, I felt, and you could hear his confidence grow with each line. "This is Wade, from the other day, just staying in range. I'm expecting to arrive around—"

He shot me a don't-blow-this look. I don't know how you ask for a ride with your eyes, but he did.

"Ten tomorrow. If anything changes, the management can reach me at *this number*—" Already I'd pressed my reporter's notepad against the glass, and he read the scribbled digits in perfect stride—a little tremulous, but no worse than other people's outdoor voices might sound with traffic going by.

At the AA meeting, Wade seemed transformed, evangelical—a ballroom butterfly in a disaster zone. This was a co-ed group in Chinatown, heavy with newcomers. Whoever wasn't in the emotional barrel was trying to get laid. A dazed-looking single mom with a bicycle helmet, off Ritalin just a couple of months, was talking with crazed intensity to a very nervous film editor who always wore stovepipe Levi's and a letterman's jacket. When she drifted away, Wade seized the other's arm. "Are you giving that chick a ride home, or what?"

"Well, I mean, she's got her bike," the editor began.

"Oh, Lord, her eyes, the way she looked at you? And she doesn't wear makeup or nothing!" Wade must have jived like this with buddies back in Denver.

But everyone knew this woman had some kind of processing disorder, and that the editor was stuck on his (happily remarried) ex-wife. *Not the love note again,* people whispered, whenever he unfolded it from his pocket during the sharing portion of the meeting. Half the room got up to fill their coffee.

"If she knew how he felt about her, she'd come back," Wade opined later, smoking at the curb. Four of us were piling in to my car, because, don't ask how, I'd been elected to give a lift to both the grieving film editor and the spellbound mom, with her bicycle jackknifed into my trunk. The bungeed hatchback bounced happily while we all debated the chances one had for remarrying one's happily remarried ex-wife. My position was straightforward: It was a poor bet. You got seemingly unending chances with women, until you got your last, and then not one chance more.

The grieving film editor agreed.

The bicycle mom said, "Right on."

It felt less hurtful if we all ganged up on Wade in sport.

But Wade pushed back. "A love letter like that? From a woman? Come on." For a woman, Wade claimed, such private admiration was rarer even than sex, or words to that effect.

"Jeez, a little sexist?" I howled. I was probably showing off to the bicycle woman.

"Oh?" Wade said. "Have *you* ever gotten a letter like that?"

"I didn't have to. I peeked at a diary entry like that." Although this possibly bolstered his point, not mine.

The car was quiet except for some dying laughter. Through the open windows, the night air only intensified Wade's scent of Irish Spring soap and Marlboro menthols, a mixture that felt specifically concocted to reawaken my depression. I would not have been shocked to hear that Wade had sprinkled himself with bathroom cleanser.

"Well, then you need to get that back too," Wade said.

"It'll be the beige building on the right," said the bicycle mom.

Watching Wade get out of the car to help the Letterman with the bicycle, I remembered what manipulation that old girlfriend was capable of—how she'd moved to LA from Boston uninvited and then made herself permanent. Then the angry person she became.

"He's walking her to the door," Wade said, climbing in again.

"Seriously. Seriously?"

He withdrew a cigarette and tapped it against my glove compartment.

"Could you please not?" I asked, adding, to make clear I was no tobacco prude, "I used to smoke three packs a day. She used to air out the room every hour when I was writing. The diary girl."

"Dell."

"Actually, this was before Dell."

"Sweet Jesus. Has anyone ever been as lucky as you?"

"Trust me, you'd have known this match was temporary. We had issues."

"Such as her airing out your studio too frequently."

"There were issues, Wade. Which I really didn't need to think about until it was all or nothing."

"Like she pressured you to get married?"

"Only silently," I said. I was saying too much. "I mean, she waited a few weeks for me to do the right thing."

He waited a long time for me to say more, and then it looked like he made a few false starts at leveling with me about something. He put the cigarette back in his pocket.

"I wonder if they're going inside," I asked, straining for a look at the letterman in the dark.

Wade was very solemn. "All right then. Did you name the unborn child?"

This was all my fault. "We never got that far."

Wade nodded and then said, as if writing a prescription, "There's a radio host named John Parker on The Fish. He's big on this subject. Your child's soul can't be at peace. It can't be released from limbo until it's got a proper name."

"How about 'Mortimer Gladwell'?"

"I'm sorry if I stepped on your toes," Wade said.

At this instant, the letterman climbed in.

"You need to do a naming ceremony for that child," Wade informed me, slipping in his last word. To the letterman: "Where are we dropping you off, my friend? As if I'd know where anything is."

"Maybe just as far as Western? My god, that girl is nuts!"

"Really? But those eyes," said Wade.

"The eyes," Letterman said. "I'll give you that."

"Do you have a candle at home to light?" Wade asked me. "I could help you with the ceremony."

Before even committing to the idea, I had nodded yes, and now I was panicking, trying either to slow this train of events or speed through the inevitable. And then we were settled at my apartment, our faces lit from beneath in the glow of a yahrzeit candle—my grandmother's, from Mount Sinai Mortuary, never used because I could never remember the date of her death.

Wade said a prayer for God's will to be done, and then invited me to do this thing—to ask the child directly, ask my unborn child its name. I sat there. His very patience was jamming me up.

"I'll go in the bathroom while you finish," he offered.

"Don't be ridiculous." I lifted the candle's tall cylinder and tiptoed across the room. I closed the bathroom door behind me reverently, placed the candle on the faux marbled counter. Heard a chilly soothing hum in the building's pipes.

How does someone's haphazardness get him from where he's been to the place he is now? While at the same time offering such strange currents of logic from the depths, flashes of a mermaid's tail, suggesting none of this has been entirely random? If only I hadn't always felt so helpless, the most extreme answers to life's problems would not have had such strange appeal to me. I would not have had that lifelong apprehension that people like Wade might be right by sheer force of their simplicity. I was thinking like this and waiting, waiting for an unborn child to tell me his name.

Or hers. Her name or his? I hadn't prepared for this question. And should I count Sylvie's first, ectopic pregnancy?

"Wade?" I called through the bathroom door.

I opened it partway, heard his halting snore—and when I returned to my candle, time had seemed to speed up. You could just tell that whatever gap Wade had opened in the physics of this night was in danger of closing, that nothing now made as much sense as leaving the bathroom, exhausted, and climbing into bed.

Half in renunciation, and half not wanting to be the guy who never misses a chance to miss a chance, I made a sort of insurance toss at the problem, flinging the name of my father's father in the direction of the past—hoping that whatever child it happened to strike was mine and Sylvie's. But I was also making up my mind that I would never again allow myself to be needy with people like Wade, no matter how earnest and special they were. Because they were only going to end up being reminders of the unbearable times during which they showed up.

———————

To explain Sylvie a bit more: She had a donkey laugh, which could relax the most insecure person in the world, and she hated her hips, a thing about her that I treasured, because something about being allowed to watch an obviously attractive girlfriend worry about her hips felt like the proof that you were living with a girlfriend. In the beginning we enjoyed watching television on hot summer nights by setting up lawn chairs outside and placing the TV set just inside the back door while we drank and drank.

But almost right away she started having symptoms. Such as: *vaginal bleeding that is heavier or lighter than your normal period,* and *sharp or stabbing pain that varies in intensity,* and a month or two later, *fevers, chills and sweats.* This was because, during my confident streak before she moved from Boston to try to make our relationship official, a series of edgy young women at Ports came on to me, one after the other, a miracle that at the time felt almost like a prank (they all knew each other, slightly), and I guess I decided that all that thoughtless liberty would be a memory I'd cherish, even in a sad way, when I got old, even with all of our innocent fighting about it, and that hasn't been untrue either.

She needed to stay a couple of extra days in the UCLA hospital to get well said the male doctor, whom I remember explaining *ectopic pregnancy* in a tone I found accusatory, but Sylvie calmed me down

184

by not liking him either, and to me the word sounded like mixing "exotic" and "tropical." I had been looking through the tinted hospital windows to the Hollywood sign and thinking: you know, we should have been hiking—how ecstatic it could be some days to live in Los Angeles and to feel absolved from guilt or shame. I was remembering a canyon hike with a very pretty artist friend, someone that Sylvie knew about, who had decided never to have children herself, because she had a congenital partial blindness that she didn't want to pass on. She could only see out of the sides of her eyes, this woman. She had waited in the street outside my building for me to get my hiking shoes, looking the wrong direction from me in order to see me, which felt silly enough to put us both in the same lighthearted mood. It was one of those days in LA when you feel like you have claim to the whole city precisely because you own none of it. I locked my front door behind me and said, genuinely at a loss, "Do we need—provisions?" It was like I suddenly wasn't sure if we'd be gone for hours or days hiking up to the Hollywood sign. And we both started laughing so hard we could barely stand.

My son Philip was born three years after these events involving Wade, and in my case, three years older was not much. Nola, his mother—a former B-movie actress whose grandparents sold auto parts in Seal Beach—made me feel I was privileging her with my heritage when I named Philip for my father's father. The fact that I'd previously given the same name away—to a child who, according to Wade, was thus freed to cavort around heaven—never rose up in my conscience as a more troubling mistake than any of countless others I'd made, at least not then.

What I can tell you is how gleamingly happy Philip seemed at age two and three—despite the premature birth, the night terrors, and the mild cerebral palsy. (He is 6'4" today, his hobbled gait only slightly evident, less cute in adulthood because one can see that it hampers him—that a great feeling of injustice hampers him.)

He seemed happy even when a vicious fight sent my wife, Nola, to her mom's for good, leaving me to try to shield my son from the knowledge of how severed every happiness thereafter would feel.

185

With depression coiled around my throat, I played with him in a mud-spattered backyard castle. We waved rusted water pistols, sailed boats in the pond of a sandbox lid. I hoisted the miracle of his body overhead, feeling his breath moist beneath his parka hood, inside which he kept disappearing to play peek-a-boo, while he yelled, "All gone, all gone!"

———————

The St. Germain Apartment Tower is stunningly restored nowadays, with high ceilings and trendy concrete floors, but in 1990s LA, it was more of a shell. Its furnished singles had fugly cream carpet and cheap linoleum and radiator heaters with dials that were drowned in white paint. Even so, we looked like crashers heading in. I had to double-park in order to unload Wade's boxes—dropping him temporarily by the main entrance with its burgundy awning. The whole edifice was built almost to the street. Finding no parking in the alley or anywhere else, I circled all the way back to double-park for a second time in five minutes, only to find that Wade was still standing exactly where I'd left him.

"I might feel better if you were with me."

"That's fine. Only let's make a pact," I said, looking up, "that one day one of us will own a hand truck."

In the dusty, tiled lobby, arms full, I veered toward the desk, but Wade was marching straight past to an elevator, so I turned heel and followed him, perhaps unwisely. The desk clerk rose, in a manner I felt I'd foreseen if not caused, and when Wade looked over his shoulder to call out, "Hi again!" the clerk looked almost purified by sadness. In any case he did not seem alarmed.

The seventh-floor room, and there were only seven floors, had a writing desk and a Murphy bed, but no chairs. Across the mantle of a faux fireplace sat a clipboard holding blank rental forms. After Wade and I slid our boxes into the corner by the sole window, he closed the door and sat down on the cream carpet against a small built-in dish hutch, his arms locked tightly around his knees, like a cosmonaut.

186

"I'm double-parked," I said, adding, "I think someone would get some good writing done here."

"How much do you want to bet this all works out?" he said, in a tone that could only be described as good-natured despair.

"You didn't even tell me it was the top floor!"

"Am I a lucky dude or what?"

I struggled to picture Wade becoming installed here, gathering the moss of a life to his form—attending city college, riding the elevator to his unit after a meeting. It was like the idea existed somewhere in the city's past or thirty years into the future, but not today.

"Stay a little longer?" he begged. "Or see you at the meeting sometime?"

"You'll get things squared away? With Mr. Elkins?"

He didn't answer.

"I'm just afraid I'll get towed," I said again, backing toward the door, and that is when the desk clerk knocked and entered. I lingered long enough to hear him ask Wade if he might prefer to come back at 3 p.m. when Mr. Elkins would arrive, and I heard Wade allow that he might grab lunch at some point if it was safe to leave his boxes where they were. All the clerk would say was, "I guess that's between you and Mr. Elkins." Then it seemed the priority was my car.

I never heard anything of Wade after that. Though I can't be positive Mr. Elkins had him removed. When I got outside, a police car approached, stopping my heart—first in fear for Wade, then for my car. Then it turned north harmlessly up Serrano. Inside, the clerk had returned to his desk. I stole one last view of the St. Germain as I drove away, my eyes scaling the façade, all the way to the top floor, where I tried to picture Wade unpacking his books in the smoggy light—the scene in my mind looked airy and elegant, yet also dated, with divans and potted plants. I wondered what other books he had stored inside his boxes. And were they all, too, about the death of beauty? I was a writer, and I'd never asked this?

To my right was the meeting hall where we'd met, and I drove past it dreaming of my future bride.

Acknowledgments

—◆—

CHARLIE HAAS, JOHN GOULD, Janet Duckworth, Sheila Finch, Gary Commins, Michele Rafael, Andrea Stein, Joe Donnelly and Steve Howard saw the novel in manuscript and gave invaluable advice. Chip Rice's devoted eye, both sentence-level and heart-level, while he was my agent, was indispensable. David Ross and Kelly Huddleston gave the book life, and a cover that I would reach for at first sight.

While the novel isn't strictly autobiographical, my children Nathan, Ben and Abby, along with an inspiring number of their generation, have absorbed in their own way how to make it okay in these times not to be okay. You are heroes.

A version of "Paper Moon" appeared online in *Angels Flight Literary West*. A version of "Double Parking at the St. Germain" appeared online in *Arlington Literary Journal*.